Hiram Munger

The Life and Religious Experience of Hiram Munger

Hiram Munger

The Life and Religious Experience of Hiram Munger

ISBN/EAN: 9783337720872

Printed in Europe, USA, Canada, Australia, Japan

Cover: Foto ©Raphael Reischuk / pixelio.de

More available books at **www.hansebooks.com**

THE LIFE

AND

RELIGIOUS EXPERIENCE

OF

HIRAM MUNGER,

INCLUDING MANY SINGULAR CIRCUMSTANCES CONNECTED WITH
CAMP-MEETINGS AND REVIVALS.

WRITTEN BY HIMSELF.

PUBLISHED AND FOR SALE BY THE AUTHOR,
CHICKOPEE FALLS, MASS.,
And at the Office of the " *Crisis,*" 167 Hanover-st., Boston
1861.

PREFACE TO THE SECOND EDITION.

In issuing a second edition of this work the autobiographer has added an Appendix containing interesting details of some of the persecutions experienced by the pioneers in the Advent faith, together with a concise narrative of subsequent labors in the year just past and gone.

The good which the Lord has been pleased to accomplish through the instrumentality of this minister is indeed great; and when we look at the wonderful revivals which have sprung up under the most discouraging circumstances wherever he went, we are ready to acknowledge that God has blessed his works abundantly in constraining sinners to come to Christ that they might have life.

The quaint originality of the style is characteristic of the man; and those who are acquainted with our brother will therein see the handiwork of the only Hiram Munger which we have, and, as Brother W——, of Albany, once said, the only Hiram Munger which we need.

The Appendix begins with a recital of a few of the trials with which our earliest preachers had to contend; and the faith of Brother Mathewson, the sufferings of Baker, and the courage of Father Hastings are touched upon in a style peculiar to the author, the perusal of which will well repay the reader.

In addition to the above, there are added a number of valuable recipes, which, to those who are so unfortunate as to require their application, are of themselves worth the price of the book; and their place there is a guaranty of their efficacy.

A lifelike portrait goes with this edition, for which we anticipate a rapid sale.

JNO. F. COTTON.

BOSTON, 1 *January*, 1861.

MUNGER'S

LIFE AND EXPERIENCE.

CHAPTER I.

In preparing this work, I must labor under many disadvantages ; first, from the fact that I cannot give but few correct dates, as I kept no journal, and most of these incidents must be given from memory for a number of years. But I will endeavor to give facts, and in some instances correct dates, and the sum and substance of circumstances, as nearly as possible.

Another difficulty which I must necessarily labor under is, omitting many names in this narrative, as many of the persons are living at this time, and many of the incidents are of such a nature, that the *names* of persons to whom they refer, being connected with the circumstances, might create sensitiveness and dissatisfaction.

This work is designed mostly to give a history of my experience in more than one hundred *camp-meetings*, and other *religious meetings*.

I have had the charge and oversight of the most
of these meetings, either directly or indirectly,
so that I felt a responsibility and duty to pre-
serve good order. This position placed me
where I necessarily came in contact with the
" Cain family," or " Children of the Devil" as
our Saviour called them. So many curious and
singular circumstances have occurred at these
meetings, that are well known to my friends,
that I have been requested to write them, as
correctly and fully as I could recollect, that
they might see them together, and have the
privilege of relating them to others. I have
objected for some years from a number of con-
siderations : one good one was that I was not
competent to produce a published work of any
kind, to appear in this age of education and criticism ; another was, I was not able to raise the
expense of publishing, and if others assisted
me, I did not want any book in the community
that was a drug to the people ; and fearing that
it might not prove interesting, I had good reasons to doubt the propriety of the undertaking.
But as we are all liable to be overcome, I will
venture, therefore, to commence and proceed as
my memory may serve me, hoping that neither
religion nor morality will suffer on its account.

I was born in Monson, Mass., September 27,
1806, of poor parents. I was the oldest son of
Stillman and Susan Munger, who were the pa-

rents of five sons and six daughters, who have all, except one, lived up to the present time, this 9th day of August, 1855. I am consequently nearly 49 years of age. There is nothing remarkable in my experience of early life any more than in that of many others. But I can recollect so distinctly circumstances that took place when I was very young, that it may refresh my memory concerning later dates to note a few things as I passed from childhood up to where I now am ; and as memory is the most I have to depend upon, it needs refreshing, and this I offer as a reason to my friends for commencing my narration previous to what they or I expected at first. I recollect a number of circumstances that took place when I was less than two and a half years of age, while living in Monson. My father moved to Ludlow in the year 1809, and tended a grist-mill for a Mr. Putman, in the place then called "Put's Bridge," since called Jenksville. While there I tended the toll-gate on the bridge. I recollect demanding the *two cents* of a colored man, who refused to pay me, and threatened me if I did not open the gate. I went for help, or to inform my father in the mill : when we came out in sight, he was on the gate (which was very high) getting over—my father shook him off, which so enraged him, that he cursed and swore at a great rate, which scared me for the first time in my life that I recollect. The same hour,

and a short distance from that place, he committed a crime worthy of death, and was executed in Northampton. His name was *Piner*.—
Many will recollect this circumstance as well as I do, for there was much excitement in that place at the time of his capture and trial.

The next work I remember doing was going into the small cotton factory over the grist-mill, started by Benjamin Jenks & Co., who came from Rhode Island. This was the first factory of that kind in Massachusetts. The help necessary to carry it on was about twelve or fifteen hands. Here was where I was first made acquainted with American slavery in the *second degree*. The treatment of the help in those days was cruel, especially to poor children, of whom I was one. Although I was young, I recollect of thinking that life must be a burden if I was obliged to work in a factory under such tyrants as the Jenks' were *then*, and they never improved, unless it was when they failed and cheated the community out of $100,000, or more, and then left the parts.

In a few years, we moved to another mill three miles north, but in the same town, and lived there three years. Here I began my education with tending grist-mill. There being few inhabitants in the place, my mother was sent for when there was any sickness, and I, being the oldest of her four children, had *all* the care when my father was absent. I remember

that my second sister was at play around the
fire, and her dress took fire ; father and mother
being gone, I tried in vain to put it out, 'till
she was very badly burned,—her screams terri-
fied the rest of the children, and no neighbors
being near, I was in a straight place sure enough.
I thought of the brook, and in an instant took
the child, and amid the screams, confusion and
fire, hastened down the bank a number of rods
through bushes and weeds, and threw her in.
The brook being large and high at the time,
she went down some distance before I could get
her out. This operation put the *fire out* and
stopped her crying, for she had strangled by
rolling over so many times while going down to
a place where I could get her out. She soon
revived, to my joy, for I was afraid that my sudden remedy was fatal. But she got well, sooner
probably by having the cold water bath. I must
have been at that time about ten years of age.
We next removed to Wilbraham, and lived a
year or so. I worked that summer for Abner
Cady, on a farm, for three dollars per month.—
This was the cold summer of 1816. My summer wages bought my father a cow, which we
kept until we moved to Chicopee, the town
where I now reside. I was now large enough to
help in the mills, and was subject to my father
for a number of years : with him I struggled
with poverty, the family now being large.

My second brother and myself were all the

help he had, to carry on a grist-mill, and some
of the time two saw-mills ; and we were so poor
that I had not clothes that were comfortable for
winter or decent for summer much of the time.
This was the misfortune of being very poor ; it
was not caused by indolence nor intemperance
of my father, for there is hardly a man that
lives, or ever *did live* or ever *will*, that worked
harder and more hours to support a family than
he did, and my mother too. I was old enough
to know that it was out of their power to do any
better by their children. But, like other boys,
I was often dissatisfied with staying at home
without clothes to go to school or meeting but
very little. I was nearly 16 years old before I
could write, or read in a paper ; and I could
not cipher at all. I was ashamed to go to school
there then, and at last got rather headstrong
and unruly, and determined to run away. I
recollect setting a time to start : got my little
all done up in a cotton handkerchief, and about
8 o'clock in the evening I started for Monson,
to my uncle's—about fifteen miles. It looked
like a great undertaking in those days. But I
started, and had got about half a mile, when
my attention was arrested by hearing some one
praying up the river about one and a half miles
from where I then was. I could hear distinctly what was said, and I staid nearly an hour and
listened, until I concluded to go back home and
put my goods in at the chamber window where

I got out. 1 went to bed thinking about that praying up the river : *that* turned my mind from running away. I staid at home peaceably for a year. I soon found out about that praying up the river. It was three old fashioned Methodists that could not have the privilege of praying in the tenement where they boarded ; this was in the upper village, now called *Chicopee Falls,* two miles from Cabotville. These men were men of God who went to work for him in good earnest. Their names were, *Carter, Patton* and *Crocker.* Their place of resort was half a mile down the river to a large, hollow *button-ball tree* where they went to pray after their day's work was done. Here was where they were when I heard them at Cabotville, which was at least one and a half miles distant. They prayed so loud and fervent that the " Cain family" found them, and commenced a violent persecution, even to the injury of their persons, but all to no purpose. These men of God were bent on something being done, and kept praying until some of their adversaries were struck like Saul of Tarsus ; some two or three in one evening.* God began to work in power, and it

---

* While these men were praying, one of the " Cain family" procured a long pole and inserting a sharp nail in the end of it, thrust it into the tree where they were praying. Instantly Patton cried out. "O Lord ! that wicked sinner has pricked me—now, Lord, prick him to the heart." The indignity was repeaied, and again he

gradually and powerfully went on in the midst
of persecution. It spread down the river, and
some were converted there, and I among them
felt the pardoning love of God and rejoiced. I
never shall forget that time. But I soon went
from there to Monson to work, and got in with
wicked young men, and, like thousands, neglected duty and got back from God. I came back
to Chicopee and staid a year or two. There I
was made acquainted with the fact that I must
pay a tax to the priest of the parish. *This* I
never had heard of ; but so it was : and so, after
all my flouncing, scolding and swearing, I had
to pay to the deacon the only fifty cents I ever
had had, or go to jail. That year a poor man's
cow was taken for the parish tax, and a young
man who was poor, had his boots attached while
they were at the shoemaker's ; and many other
similar specimens occurred in that region.—
This sickened and disgusted me with the old
fashioned way of supporting "the standing
order" by law, against our will. I heard some
talk about "signing off"* to get rid of paying a
parish tax ; and I thought if there *was* a way

cried, "O Lord, he has pricked me again, now prick him
to the heart." The prayer was heard—awful conviction
rested on the scoffing crowd, and several who were that
night convinced of sin are now able ministers of the Gospel. Behold the power of prayer.

* Persons belonging to other churches could, by certify-
ing the fact over their signature, avoid paying the regular
tax.

to get off, I should never pay Deacon Stedman another fifty cents till I got ready. I began to doubt the Christianity of all professors. Aunt Ruel Van Horn's kind of religion I thought the *best* that I ever *had* seen, and would attend meeting where she did. She was a Methodist woman who had lately come into the place, and who lived her religion out, and has ever since. She was alive last week, and I called on her and talked over the old times that we had twenty-five or thirty years ago. I found her as strong in God as ever, though now nearly seventy years old. As there is nothing of importance from this time, I shall skip a few years to come more directly at the subject of Camp-meetings.

The year that I was married, I lived in South Wilbraham and tended Wm. Moseley's mills. I heard of a Camp-meeting in Connecticut, about twelve miles from there ; and as I had never attended one, I concluded to go, and learning that the Methodists had put some into the preachers' stand for not obeying their rules, I proposed to a man of equal strength, named Goodale, to go with me, and see if the Methodists could put us into the preachers' stand. I had never seen a preachers' stand at this time. We arrived in sermon time, and got a sight at the stand, but concluded that it would not be a stand, or *standing* long, if they put another man into it. In the afternoon, while the committee was trying to get the men to take their *side* of the ground, we broke over their rules, determined to do as we pleased, and did, and were able to carry it out as far as masculine strength was necessary, for probably it would have needed a great number to have got either of us into the stand. Our conduct in disobeying and traveling where we pleased seemed to suit a class, that had been somewhat disturbed by the committee the day before, and seeing our determination to persist in our course, and break over their rules, these rowdies thought they had got additional strength ; so when evening came there was a mob assembled to tear down tents, and do other mischief. But Goodale and myself kept back. The mob assembled, expecting us to assist them in their operations, but as we had been treated better by the Methodists than we had treated them, we had no disposition to injure them. The mob commenced their operations, and great confusion followed ; women and children were screaming, some were fighting, and Kilburn, the presiding elder, called on every man to help protect the encampment from this wicked mob, and all that were interested on either side came together ; but we looked on and had no part or interest on either side. But human nature is of such material that it will take sides in *sympathy* if nothing more, sooner or later. In a short time I saw the mob had began to use clubs, and had struck old father Henry (as he was called)—one of our townsmen—and the blood was running down his face. "Who struck you?" said some one. "I don't know, but God knows," said he. He called for help, and I couldn't be an idle spectator any longer. I told Goodale it was time for us to interfere. So we both agreed to take sides with the Methodists, as they had been shamefully treated and abused. We told them to come on, and some of them followed. The scuffle was near a bush-fence, and we went into the merits of the case very suddenly, and began throwing them over the bush-fence, and they soon saw something very different from what they had expected, for we made short work— took a number, and the rest ran—and we stayed on the ground and protected it during the rest of the night. The mob dare not return, and did not during the rest of the meeting. In this case, God turned the hearts of two wicked men to his glory.

So much for the first Camp-meeting I ever saw or attended.

The next year I moved back to Chicopee to a place called Willimansett, and took a saw-mill. There I heard Wilbur Fisk preach for the first time. I recollect people thought much of the preaching. I soon heard Fisk and Orange Scott preach at Hadley Falls, two miles north of Willimansett; then I was convinced of being a wicked backslider, but kept it to myself, and stopped going to meeting. Soon after,

Priest Phenix, (so-called), a Congregationalist,
had an appointment in the school-house (near
where I lived) for a temperance meeting. I
was persuaded to go although I had a prejudice
against him, for it was his deacon who took the
fifty cents out of me for the parish tax, a year
or two before. But I went to meeting and
heard his argument in favor of temperance.—
His reasoning was better than I expected. He
was very zealous, and tried to get names on the
temperance pledge. He failed in the first at-
tempt, but he discovered that a number in the
house referred to me, and said if he would get
me to sign they would. The old man came to
me and ventured to ask me to sign the pledge.
I told him I was not a drunkard, and other
arguments that caused him to give me up for
that time. He kept trying others, and again
came to me privately, and asked me if I knew
that I stood in the way of his success in that
place. I told him no ; they were all of age
and could act for themselves. He persuaded
and I argued. At last he wanted to know if I
thought my signing the pledge would be the
means of saving one man, I would do it. I
told him I could not *then*, for I had got three
gallons of rum at home which I must drink, and
other like excuses. But the old man did not
like to give it up without having one sign the
pledge in that place, and so he tried me on another tack, to know if I would sign for one

month. This was in July, and I thought it was necessary to keep out *heat*, and keep off sickness, &c. He did not give up then, but told me if I would sign the pledge, he believed *others* would be saved from a drunkard's grave, if *I* was not, and appealed to my conscience to know if I would not make the small sacrifice of stopping drinking spirit for *one month* for the sake of others being saved from a drunkard's grave. I told him if I had any evidence that it *would*, I would stop. He said *he* had the evidence that it would. I finally told him that for his sake and his faith, I would sign that evening, with the understanding that if I could not stand it a month, I would take my name off in a week or two, if I chose. He agreed to it, and to the astonishment of others, I signed the pledge, then took the paper and demanded the names of those who agreed to sign if I would, and got them to sign. And a good many signed the pledge that evening ; none, however, upon conditions but myself ; this was a *secret bargain* between us alone. Next day I was called a " cold water man," &c. Time passed on *one* week, and I did not drink any of my cherry rum that I had just made, although I expected to ; for I meant to get my name off the pledge soon. One day I thought I would take it off, but Priest Phenix had carried the pledge home with him : so I thought I would stand it till I could see him without going three miles to his house ;

the cherry rum tempting me every day. I got
sick of my bargain, and meant to see him that
day, but something hindered me. I heard that
he was going to have a temperance meeting in
lower Chicopee the next evening, and thought
I would go, and then have my name taken off.
The old man was there, full of zeal and faith
that he should succeed in getting signers to the
pledge. I could not see him till the meeting
was over. Then, to my astonishment, he took
out the pledge, and showed the people what he
had done up at Willimansett, and my name
was first. This looked bad to me, as I had
come four miles to get my name off the pledge,
but to have it exhibited in public, and in my
old place of residence, was a set-back, sure
enough. To go to him *then* to get my name
off, was something that I would not do, if the
cherry rum stood untouched till doomsday. A
number signed that evening under my name,
and there was a society formed on the spot, and
three men were nominated to circulate the
pledge, and I was the first, and was voted in.
This was turning things about in a hurry.—
What to do I did not know. There I was
down for the purpose of getting out of the collar, but I had got into the *harness* sure enough.
I had too much pride to let my business be
known then, so I took the pledge and went to
work, thinking, perhaps I might do somebody
some good, and could erase my name when I

pleased. I got a great number of names, many
more than I expected. On going home, the
cherry rum was in my way, and for me to be
offering the pledge to others, and keeping the
liquor in the house, looked to me hypocritical ;
so I got rid of the three gallons at once, bidding
it farewell forever. I then felt better in every
respect, for I had not drank a drop for about
three weeks, and was conscious that it was doing no harm at least. I now had an inclination
to attend meetings, which I had not done only
occasionally for a number of years ; and I believe
the hand of God was in this movement, and perhaps the man I was so much prejudiced against
(for having received the fifty cents paid to him
from his deacon) was the instrument in the hand
of God of good to me. At any rate, I commenced with a pledge of a month, and have kept it
twenty-five years. I have never seen him to
speak to him since, for he soon moved off ; but
if he should be living, and should see this book
with this fact, he may know that his labor in
the temperance cause has been blessed in some
degree at least. All that I am acquainted with,
who signed the pledge that first evening, have
kept it to this day : and we have talked it over,
and looked at it as being a great and wise step
for us, for we are still willing to make a sacrifice
for the cause of temperance in all its phases, and
risk the stigma that may result therefrom.

The next year I moved from Willimansett

back to lower Chicopee, and added over two hundred names to the pledge, and felt justified in *that*, but condemned before God, for I was a *backslider*. The meeting was still kept up, and had been ever since the three men of God first assembled in the hollow tree, a few years before. By this time the Methodists had gained a foothold, and built a small chapel, and had meetings every Sabbath. I attended, and soon became interested in them, and had a desire, like David, to have God restore unto me the joys of his salvation. I tried every way to get relief, but was determined to keep my feelings to myself, until I got what I was seeking after; and month after month I tried every possible way that I could think of to please God. I would get all the people that I could out to meeting, and often would take them into my boat and carry them there, hoping to do some good thing in this way to please God, and come into his favor by good works. I kept getting signers to the temperance pledge, and in fact I did penance enough in various ways to satisfy a Catholic priest, but all to no purpose; things grew worse all the while. I was determined to get blessed before I let my feelings be known, even to my wife. I finally concluded that I would rise for prayers when a good and convenient opportunity presented itself. I attended all the meetings, and at this time the meetings were very interesting, as there was a revival going on all the while in the Methodist chapel. I heard different preachers, Scott, Fisk, White, Stephens, and many others, and did not find a convenient time to go forward all this time.

There was a great deal of persecution, for the "Cain family" acted like their father the Devil, and I made up my mind I would act as regulator, and keep order at the meetings at least, and defend God's people, for my sympathy was with them. I prosecuted some twelve or fifteen in a short time ; some were overseers in the factories, others were members of other churches. Some I pitched out of the house ; others who had been stoning the meeting-house I followed half a mile, and caught them, &c., thinking perhaps that I was in some way at work for God's people, if nothing more. Many a time I have stayed out in secret places to catch those who came to disturb the meeting ; and some will long recollect the brief interviews we had a short distance from the Methodist chapel. But enough on this point.

The reformation still continued, but I found no convenient time to go forward. I remember well the hardest time I ever had to keep my seat was when a young convert testified, and told her simple story of what God had done for her, and the tears ran freely at the same time. This was one of the daughters of father Carter, so called, one of the first three who commenced working for God down under the old button-ball tree that I have mentioned before. She talked and cried, and talked till the sharp arrows of the Almighty stuck fast in many hearts, mine for one. None of the great guns that had been fired at me before touched the tender place as that small stone out of the little sling did. I then agreed, with two others, to go forward for prayers the next time there was an invitation. The time came, and the question arose who should start first. I mention this to show others the need of individual decision in matters of religion. Neither would be first, and so we all sat still that evening. The next evening some of my *friends* were present, and it was not convenient *then*, and I saw that the Devil would have something in the way as long as I was undecided ; and I made up my mind, that if all the whole *world* was present I would go forward the next evening. The time came, and I *hoped* that my friends would not be there, but it seemed that all of them knew what I had determined to do, and came to see if they could not laugh me out of it ; and they *would* have done it, had I not decided *wholly* that I would make the trial that night. I recollect that Bro. Josiah Litch called upon all to come forward who felt the need of prayers. My heart thumped and fluttered, until I thought every person in the house heard it. I finally arose and went to the front seat, and to my surprise, others whom I supposed had come in to *hinder*, came forward and took a seat with me, and some whom I had previously had hold of, all which helped to break me down before God. Brother Litch and others prayed fervently for us ; some came out clear, and I felt better at the close of the meetings. While going home, I determined to serve God if I was damned ; and while walking along in the road I lifted my heart to Him for His blessing. All at once I had such peace break in upon my mind that I stopped still.— I dare not shout, for the road was full of people, so I got away alone in some bushes, on the bank of the river, and if ever any body was happy it was me. I praised God, I laughed, I cried, I shouted, and then tried to pray, but I could not ask for any thing, for I had then got *every thing*. I never found so delightful a place before. I staid there until midnight, all alone, yet with the best company I ever had. I could not sleep after I got to my boarding place.

Now commences my Christian experience.— I was about twenty-five years of age. I will give a short sketch of my experience along a few years, for the purpose of assisting others who have had similar feelings, and fallen in time of trial in consequence of not going forward in duty. The great blessing which I had got continued for a number of days, and in this time my wife was converted. I worked away from home with a gang of hands wicked as Satan himself. I felt it duty to exhort them to seek God.

But the cross was very great, as the " boss" was
wicked, and I thought he would turn me away
if I ventured to introduce a subject so odious to
him as religion.   So I gave up the idea at that
time, and thinking that I should have a more
favorable opportunity, I kept to work with them.
At last I got in the dark, and then I could do
duty of no kind.   This continued for a week.
The preacher informed us that there was going
to be a camp-meeting down at Haddam, and he
wanted to get a certain number to go.   I put
my name down for two, thinking it a good place
for me to get out into liberty again.   The time
came, and about four hundred of us started on
a small steamboat for Haddam, a distance of seventy miles down the Connecticut river.   Many
will recollect that time : the journey was tedi-
ous.   We arrived on the ground at midnight ;
there was no tent up, and we had to lay in the
woods.   Next day we pitched the tent.   We
were all tired out, and had no enjoyment : my
wife was homesick, and my little boy fell into
the fire and burned himself very badly, and it
did seem as though " the devil was to pay" all
around.   I could not get home, for the boat did
not go under a week from then.   I saw that I
could not live so, and I went forward for prayers
every time there was an invitation, and that was
a number of times a day, for God's people were
in the work, and sinners were converted at every
meeting.   But I grew harder and more indif-

ferent. Prayer didn't touch my case ; but I
kept going forward, until a preacher (I wish I
knew where he was) came to me in the prayer-
circle, and said that he had observed me there
a number of times, and wished me to tell him
how I felt. I told him I had no feelings and
wanted to get some. He then wanted me to
relate my experience, which I did a year or two
back. He then gave me such instructions as I
needed : he told me it would do me no good to
go forward for prayers : I had neglected duty,
and fallen into darkness in consequence of it.—
God blessed me for taking up the first cross, and
condemned me for neglecting the second. He
talked plain and I felt the force of his words.—
He recommended to me a class-meeting in which
to tell my feelings and experience, and I should
feel better. This was another cross, as I had
never yet spoken in meeting ; but I followed
his advice, and the Lord blessed me again ; and
always after that I found obedience was better
than sacrifice. During the remainder of this
meeting, I felt at home. I had attended a number of camp-meetings before, but always as a
spectator until now. There was one circumstance that took place worthy of note. There
was a gambler went forward for prayers, without any conviction, to gratify his praying sister
who was there. I saw him go, and knew him,
and had known him from a boy. He went down
on the boat and confessed he was going to gam-

ble. I kept watch of him to see what effect
prayer would have upon him : he laughed out
quite heartily once or twice in derision, seeing
others slain, till at last he was slain, and cried
for mercy in such distress of mind as I never
heard before nor since. His old comrades for-
sook him and ran. He was in such a state of
mind and plead so earnestly for mercy, that all
efforts to appease him and keep him still were
in vain. Even when the bell rung for the preaching, the congregation could not be gathered to
the stand, the Presiding Elder left the stand
and came to the tent where he was, and tried to
comfort and still him ; but his agony was so
great, and his entreaties so cutting to the people, that the elder said God was at work in a
mysterious way, and there would be no preaching *that* afternoon. So all went to their tents
for prayer-meetings, and many were converted.
He found peace, and from that day to this never doubted the power which God's people had
over him in prayer. While coming up on the
boat, he fell off the deck and sprained his ancle.
The doctor who was aboard pronounced it a very
bad sprain. It was badly swollen, and very
painful. He told some of his friends, if they
would pray, he believed the pain would cease
and the swelling go down. He insisted, and
prayer was offered, the crew all eager to see if
the thing would be done. I among many doubted the effect of the medicine ; but they prayed,

and he said the pain ceased : at any rate, the swelling went down immediately, and *I saw it*. He could add much to this circumstance, if he was here ; for he is yet alive, and believes still in the God of Israel as having all power. I omit his name ; but G. M. will affirm this as being true, and many others will recollect it. Nothing else of importance occurred while on the boat, and we all returned home in safety with more than twenty converts. The work spread in every direction, and with such power as astonished many people.

Two facts I will relate. In the town of Ludlow, in time of a powerful revival, two men opposed the work, and a friend of theirs who was present at one of the meetings, requested prayers for them. The church prayed for them as though they had been present ; but they were a number of miles off, and knew nothing of it. God answered their prayers, and one of them, an old man by the name of Collins, who was ploughing, was stricken down, and, as I understood, lay helpless for some time. I have seen him many times, and heard him testify to the goodness of God, and His power to save the hardest of sinners, of whom he was one. The other man was cutting bushes, and *he* was struck down in the field, and gave *his* heart to God, and I think he told me that he went from the field to the meeting-house before going home. He said many more things ; but I have partly forgotten them, therefore I only write what I distinctly remember. God worked in mysterious ways in those days. This was when *Methodists* stood in the liberty and faith of the gospel, and craved more for the salvation of souls, than they did for fine houses and fine clothes. Those times were before the devil dared offer to come into a Methodist church with his fiddle under his arm, for he and everybody else knew them as far as they could see or hear them, and that was a great distance.   ʊ

There was another circumstance worthy of note, which took place about this time among the " Cainite" generals, or " Hagarenes." See Ps. lxxxiii : 5-6. A confederacy was entered into by some three or four of the upper *ten*, to break up the Methodists before they got too strong a hold in the village. The agent was considered a powerful man, and when he undertook anything, it was done. His edict had gone forth, that he would stop praying in the tenements on the corporation ground, or he would turn away every one that broke his great command. The fear of *God* (instead of man) is the beginning of wisdom. The people began to pray to God to take the agent in hand, and let the reformation go on. Soon it broke out anew. One family ventured to obey God rather than man, broke the rules of the agent, and held a meeting that lasted *all day*. It went in power, and a number were converted. One was the daughter of old father Carter, one of the three who commenced holding meetings under the old button-ball before alluded to. She came out alive, 'and like old Deborah, waited for no *man*, when God called *her* to do duty. She had an interview with the agent, told him what God had done for her, and by so doing gained a victory over him and his father the devil.— She went back into the factory, and kept at work for the agent and for God. She could do double the work after she got such victory. The work spread in the factory ; the agent swore, and commenced putting his threats into execution by turning away all those who had ventured to have praying in his tenements after he had objected. One afternoon, about two o'clock, he started for the blacksmith's shop, where two of God's servants were at work, to give them notice to leave. Two of the girls in the factory saw him going, and knew his errand, and called upon God to stop him in his course. One of them said that while she was looking at him when he came within a few rods of the shop, he fell to the ground like a dead man. She spoke to the other, and said, " God has taken Hanshaw in hand." She told me recently that she knew God answered their prayers on the spot. The men ran and picked their powerful agent up, and carried him home. Poor Saul, God stood in his way, and he didn't do his errand. A council of doctors was called, but no one knew what ailed him—they all called it *a strange case.* He lay in this condition about *three months,* and the work of God spread so extensively that he could do nothing with so many converts. Even if he had wished to, I think he had found it hard to kick against the pricks ; at any rate, he never tried it after that. This circumstance will be recollected by Otis Wait's wife, John Miller and his wife, and many others whom I have forgotten. This is the way God used to demonstrate his regard for that people. But see them now. Said a Methodist preacher to me the other day : " Bro. Munger, we can never expect to bring Methodism back again on the ground where it once was." Sure enough, it is not destined to go back, but foreward ; and those who have stopped to play by the way, with the trifling toys of this world, have become like the nations or neighbors around them, lost sight of the old paths, and got back into the dark ; and to bring the doctrines back there is impossible, "for," says John Wesley, " when this people cease to carry out their principles, God will raise another people, who *will* carry them out, and go forward, and not back."

This new fashioned way of worship did not suit *me* nor any of the old fashioned Methodists. About the time that the fusion of the world and Methodist church commenced, a circumstance took place which it may not be amiss to men-

tion. There was a protracted meeting in Chicopee Falls, and the preachers mostly came from
the "minister factory," in Wilbraham. They
were young, but very *neat* and particular, as is
generally the case. There was one who was
very much so. He preached a number of even-
ings, not hitting the heart, nor even the head
of any. His charges were spent in the air.—
Nobody laughed—nobody cried ; but those who
kept him over night muttered about how much
trouble he made them. His bed must be very
nice, and his room well furnished in city style.
His food must be served with the greatest care,
or he would make some remark telling them how
he lived in Boston. He took occasion to let the
people know that he had been an *actor* in a the-
atre, which accounted for his accomplished ges-
tures in the desk, and his way of living, and lying in bed so late ; for he would lie in bed until
called to breakfast, and then want cold and warm
water brought into his room, with two or three
towels, hindering the family half an hour or more
preparing his dignity with pomatum or some
other perfumery. This was a great trouble in
a factory village where people had to be govern-
ed by bell hours. The brethren and sisters got
tired of him in one day, and no one wanted to
keep this dandy preacher. One of the brethren,
I think it was Rufus Baker, came to me to have
me keep him over night. I told him that I
would take him, if he could travel half a mile

in the mud, up to my house. He consented,
as no one else gave him an invitation. We started, Indian-file : I went ahead in a path, and
travelled as usual at a good gait. We soon arrived at home. My wife and children were in
bed, it being late. I was accustomed to have
something to eat before going to bed. I took
out the table drawer on to my knees, and took
hold of the cold boiled victuals, gave him a knife
and fork, and told him that he was welcome.—
He hesitated a little, but finally took hold. After supper, I gave him a candle, and told him
where to sleep, and *I* went to bed. Got up in
the morning, did my chores, and, when breakfast
was ready, we sat down to eat, without calling
him. He heard the dishes rattle, and us eating,
so he got up and came out of his room just as
we were finishing our breakfast. He said he did
not observe any accommodation for washing in
his room. I told him there was a good skillet out
at the well and a towel behind the door. I discovered that his dignity was dashed ; but my ac-
commodations were good enough for *me* and the
presiding elder, and other preachers of the old
stamp, and it was good enough for him, if he
had been an *actor*. I had my horse harnessed
and must leave him soon. I told my wife to ask
him to pray after he had finished his breakfast.
I left him eating with the children. I never saw
him after that—before night he was gone. He
quit the meeting and the place, and was no more

trouble to any one *there*. I heard that he went
directly back to Wilbraham to finish his education. If his eyes happen to light upon this
page, he will recollect the little red house about
half a mile east of Chicopee Falls, where this
took place. I live in the same village yet, and
keep a pilgrim's home. I am yet as partial as
ever to dandy preachers. Please call.

This G. M., of whom I have already spoken,
was known for years as the noisy man, and he
was rightly named, for I saw him when he was
struck down, and he began his noise then and
kept it up for years. He had family prayers,
and all in the village who lived within half a
mile of him had to hear praying *once* a day at
least. One man said that he had to get through
before Miller began, or wait, for he could not
hear himself, and their houses were eighty rods
apart or more. It was unusual, in those days,
for him to have a boarder in his tenement a
month without getting him or her converted.
But I will not multiply words on this strange
subject. To some of our modest and modern
professors, these things are unknown, and they
would be surprised to hear any one say that they
had seen thousands cut down (as before mentioned) at camp-meetings and other meetings,
and among other denominations, when they
would let God work in his own way. I am not
writing this work to suit politicians, sectarians,
grammarians, or musicians. I only expect to

touch different subjects as they come in my way
and to my mind, while passing along. To relate
what I have experienced is the design of this
book, without running into others views any
more than I consider needful to do what I think
is justice to the different subjects on which I
shall hereafter speak. I shall pass some years
now, by simply saying that I joined the Methodist church nearly twenty-five years ago, and
had a great many good meetings with them, but
always was opposed to instrumental music being
brought into the house of God. I thought it
belonged to the other family, i. e., the " Cain
family," and it was always used by the other
family at the dedications of idols, see Gen. iv :
21, and you will see that instruments were first
used by the sons of Jubal, the grand-son of
Cain. I would to God they had always *remained* in the " Cain family" where they belonged ;
but by this time perhaps the fiddlers in Zion are
touched, and run to David to be justified, because *he* used them. So he did, and Uriah's
wife too, and disobeyed God in so doing, and Nathan reproved him ; and if you read Ps. li : 11-
15, you will see him in a backslidden state
of mind in consequence. Then read Amos v :
21-24, and you will see how God hated songs
that had the sound of the viol in them. Next
read Amos vi : 1-5, and you will observe what
state the professed people of God were in when
they commenced fiddling. They were *at ease*

in Zion, and God reproved them, and mentioned the sin of David for inventing instruments of music. Read it, you church fiddlers : then look at his son Solomon, after he acknowledges he has *backslidden,* see how he went into instruments of music and other fooleries. See Eccl. ii : 7-8 ; here he had musical instruments of all sorts. Look at Job, and you will see that he says great men are not always wise men. Now if you can make anything out of David or Solomon, when God has in so many places condemned it by his Word, you may. I have not quoted half of the passages where the Lord has directly spoken or frowned upon it. And every man of God knows by his experience when the work of God is going on, that this trash of the sons of Jubal, grates upon their ears. Even the old king Darius, when he was under conviction for the wicked act of putting Daniel into the lion's den, sent the fiddlers all away, and would not have any instruments of music come before him the night that Daniel was in the den. Why ? God was at work upon his mind ; and no man ever did have an appetite for such stuff, when the Spirit of God was at work as it was with the king at that time. Read Dan. vi : 18, 19, 20, and you will see that God had been at work with the king all night : and he did not want the " Cain family" about him, and he got rid of them the next day, thank God. A few more thoughts on this point and I will close. Look at the inconsistency of the Church that will not let a wicked man take part in their social meetings, nor pray around their altars, nor servo their tables on sacramental occasions, much less to go into the desk publicly and take the lead of worshippers. Why not ? Why, he is not a professor, and is not fit. Now, for my part, I think the *house* of God is designed for the *people* of God to worship in ; and the desk is no more sacred than the orchestra in and of itself. All are dedicated alike to God ; and *singing* is as much worshipping, as *praying* or *preaching* ; and common sinners would not be allowed to preach or asked to pray ; but the meanest and most abandoned characters, and publicly known as such, are *invited*—yea, more, they are *hired* to take a part in the service of God, and they *lead* too. Many times this is a common thing. No questions are asked, only " Is he a good player ?" No wonder God will not smell in your solemn assemblies ; they stink with the instruments and spirit of the " Cain family," and he says so, as before quoted in Amos. I think David uttered a correct sentiment, as seen in the last verse of the last Psalm, " Let every thing that hath *breath* praise the Lord." So I say, and the *organs* that God has *created* to praise him are the very ones which I am contending for, and when put in tune by the Author of their being, they will be acceptable worship, and the singing will be in the spirit and with the understanding ; *not* solemn words and a thoughtless tongue, as is the case in thousands of instances. Many times it is more trouble to manage a small choir of singers, than a church of hundreds—why ? because they do not, as a general thing, enjoy religion, yet they take such a prominent part in the worship of God, that they do not feel under any obligations to any one in the church. Why should they, when the church is so very dependent upon them ? Many of the choirs are a nest of unclean birds, tolerated and supported by the church. The foregoing are a part of the reasons why I hate instuments of music in the professed house of God, and by telling my views plainly, while in the Methodist church, I caused the fiddlers in Zion and those that sympathized with them, to come down on me with the spirit of the " Cain family," and I never felt at home there after that.*

I will now give some account of the great camp-meeting in Chicopee Falls in 1842. In

* That my views on instrumental music are not new, will be shown by the following, from Dr. Jennings, of England.

" The use of instrumental music in public worship was one of the typical ceremonies of the Jewish religion, which is *abrogated*, therefore, with the rest by the gospel dispensation; and there is *no revival of this institution* in the New Testament. The *ancient fathers* were so far from practising or approving instrumental music in Christian worship, that some of them would hardly allow it was *used* in the *Jewish* : but put allegorical interpretations on the texts that mention it. St. Basil calls musical instruments the *invention of Jubal, of the race of Cain*. And *Clement of A'exandria* says, they are better for *beasts* than *men*. That musical instruments were *not used* even in the *popish church*, in Thomas Aquinas' time, about

the summer of '42, Bro. Reuben Ransom, the
presiding Elder, wished to know where I wanted
the annual camp-meeting that fall, as I had
attended every one, for years, and so many times
found fault with the location and management,
he was going to let me select the spot and manage the financial affairs of the meeting. I hesitated a while, for I knew that my way would
be peculiar to myself and very different from
what he might expect. My father had said many

the year 1250, appears from this passage in his questions : ' In
the old law, God was praised both with musical instruments
and human voices; but the Christian Church does *not* use
instruments to praise Him, lest she should seem to Judaize.'
So that it seems instrumental music hath been *introduced*
into Christian worship, within about the last *five hundred years*,
in the *darkest* and most CORRUPT *times* of POPERY. It is re-
tained in the Lutheran church, *contrary* to the opinion of *Lu-
ther*; who, as Eckard confesses, reckoned organs among the
ENSIGNS OF BAAL. Organs are still used in some of the Dutch
churches; but *against* the *minds* of their *pastors*; for in the
National Synod at Middleburgh, 1581, and in that of Holland
and Zealand, 1594, it was resolved, that they would endeavor
to obtain of the magistrates, the laying aside of *organs*, and
the singing with them in churches. The Church of England
also, in her homilies, strongly remonstrates against the use of
organs and other *instruments* of music in churches. In the
homily on the place and time of prayer, after mention of
pipeing, singing, chanting, and playing on organs, which was
in use before the reformation, we are exhorted ' greatly to rejoice, and give thanks to God, that our churches are *deliv
ered* out of these things, that *displeased God so sore*, and so
filthily defiled the holy *house* and place of prayer.' I only add,
that the voice of *harpers* and *musicians*, and of *pipers* and
trumpeters, is mentioned among the glories of mystical *Baby-
lon*, ' that *mother* of *harlots* and *abominations* of the earth,
whom God will destroy with the sword of his mouth, and
with the brightness of his coming, Rev. xviii: 22." JENNINGS'
JEWISH ANTIQUITIES, B. 1, chap. v; pp 193, 194.

times that I always had a way of my own and different from others, which of course was "bred in the bone." In July, I think, Elder Ransom and some eight or ten other preachers, came to my house as usual to talk over the affairs about the prosperity of Zion and camp-meetings, &c., and it was decided for me to go ahead and locate the meeting, and I consented. In a short time I selected a grove a short distance from the village, took the leases of the different pieces of land adjoining, which were eight or nine I think, and appointed the meeting the 15th of August. This arrangement disappointed the Elder, and he made haste to see me, for this was a new thing ; the meeting was two or three weeks *earlier* than usual, and exactly in the vicinity of rowdyism, therefore he could not become reconciled to it, and obtained some of the preachers' opinions, and *they* were astonished also, and opposed the location and time. I then gave my *reasons* for such a course, which were as follow :

First—We had always held our meetings the first week in September, and it was wet and cold, and we should shun that by this arrangement.

Second—We had always gone from ten to twenty miles from home, and generally as far from any village or house as possible, for the sake of getting away from the devil, as we used to say, and the stonier and muddier the road

the better.   Some will recollect this fact, who
went, the year before, to *Pelham*, and it appeared to me, that if we had the rowdies among
the citizens, they would not act as bad at *home*
as abroad.   I gave other reasons, and argued my
case as well as I could.   He finally concluded
that, as I had taken the leases, and had gone
so far, and had such confidence in the community, that I might *try* the experiment, but *he*
expected to be torn all up, and I must bear the
responsibility.   He doubted whether the brethren would dare come with their tents and families ; he went off feeling bad, poor man, and I
felt bad on his account, and would have abandoned it, had I not got so far along, for I had
heard others scold, saying, I had got the devil's
ground, because I had the ground of Elihu
Adams the tavern-keeper.   But I had got to
try the experiment, and as this was the first
meeting that I had ever had charge of, I put
the best foot forward, seated the ground, and
some of the preachers fell in with me ; one
preacher, Bro. Phio Hawks, for the first one,
Bro. W. Ward next, and so on, until the fears
of the Elder were somewhat lessened.   The
time came for the meeting, and the people came
from every direction, and Monday night sixty
tents were pitched, and five more Tuesday ;
some of the tents were very large, the boarding tent was 100 feet long, and 22 wide, and
the lodging tent for strangers, was 110 feet

long and 20 wide. The meeting progressed
harmoniously Tuesday and Wednesday. There
was another new thing ; I let the *pedlers* into
the ground that I had taken the lease of, within fifty rods of the camp. The Elder used
to drive them back a *mile*, to the extent of the
law. This always made them mad, and they
did not care how much the rowdies *did* trouble
us. I tried this experiment on my own hook,
by first letting them know the law, and then
giving them such privileges that they felt under
obligations to us and promised to help protect
the meeting. The rowdies had to pass the
pedlers' stands to get to the camp ground, and
finding the pedlers all still and quiet, and so
near the ground, it created a surprise, and they
inquired of the pedlers what this meant ? They
told them that the ground belonged to the encampment, and they were there by the permis-
sion of the Committee, on condition that there
should be no strong drink sold, nor any noise
from rowdies, and they should go against every
thing that would disturb the meeting. The rowdies in that vicinity were headed in this way in
part : then Adams, the tavern-keeper, was deputy sheriff, and the rowdies there were known
by him and me, and they knew that I would
put "Cæsar's dogs" on their track if they did
not behave. So you see the whole machinery
or arrangement was new, but it worked well,
and the meeting was one of the most quiet that

was ever held in New England, although the
largest that I ever attended. Every one said,
they never attended such a meeting before, and
even the Elder was so happily disappointed, that
he proposed holding it over the Sabbath, and
they all agreed to it, a thing which they never
did before or since, to *my* knowledge. Over
one hundred were reported to have been converted at this meeting; it truly was a great
and good meeting, if I *did* venture out on a
new plan of operation. All were satisfied with
it. We had no difficulty with the "Cain family" worth mentioning at this meeting.

About Friday or Saturday, Bro. Stebbins and
R. E. Ladd told me that the Millerites wanted
the ground the next week, and wanted the seats
to stand. They were going to pitch the largest
tent that I ever saw, in the centre of the ground.
I did not think much of it, for I had heard Miller preach one half day at Three Rivers, and he
whipped the churches so hard, that I was sore
then, and I felt off about it. Next came Elihu
Adams and J. V. Himes to see me. Adams
owned the ground, and was anxious to let the
Millerites have it. I believe Himes offered him
$25 for the privilege and use of the preacher's
stand and seats ; but I felt crusty, and objected. As I had luckily taken all my leases for
the month of August, it was not Adams' to let
until September ; and I owned the lumber and
slabs, so I had a good chance to act " the dog

in the manger," and keep off the Millerites.—
But Adams, Stebbins, Ladd, and I *think*, *Himes*
all came again, and offered *me* the $25 towards
defraying the expenses of our meeting, which
were about $200. This was an object ; and as
Bros. Ladd and Stebbins (who were brethren I
thought much of) were anxious, and Bro. Hawks
did not oppose, I consented to give the leases
over to any one whom they chose, the next Tuesday, as our meeting broke up Monday. The
next *Monday* they all came to see me again, and
Himes wanted I should agree to keep on through
the next meeting, as I had my hand in, and keep
the leases and officers that I had, and for my
services offered me $25. After consulting my
brethren, I agreed to that also, and Himes wanted all the tents to stand—boarding tent, lodging tent, and all. I thought he looked like a
man that ought to know better than that ; but
I had enlisted ; so I went to work to see how
many would let their tents stand through the
next meeting ; and I found that nearly all would
if I would be responsible for their safety, which
I agreed to, Himes backing me up. After our
meeting closed, and all went home, it looked lone-
some. The tents stood empty, and I had to
watch them two days and nights ; for their
meeting was to commence Thursday, the 26th.
Their large tent came Wednesday, and a lot of
hands commenced cutting down the trees in the
grove. This looked like sacrilege to me : I was

sorry that I had enlisted. All of my old brethren were gone, and a new set of people there,
and all the responsibility of the tents on me.—
But I could not back out, so I went to work.
When they showed me the length of the tent-
pole they wanted, I was more astonished than
ever : it was to be 55 ft. high. The pole was
procured, and I helped raise it ; and their workmen commenced to raise the tent. The novel-
ty of the scene drove off my blues, for the tent
covered all our seats, and a rod all around, besides. It was 25 rods around it—I never saw
half so large a tent before. I, and others, *thought*
and *said*, " Where are all the people coming
from to fill it ?" for it was estimated to hold
from 3000 to 4000. The meeting commenced
with a few, and all strangers except a *very* few.
The meeting was so different from the other that
I took but little interest in it—excepting the
$25, and I hoped that they would not make out
much. The next day many more came : the
preaching was very good. Bros. Stoddard, Kenny
and Collins came on, and I found that *they* were
believers. The next day a great multitude
came, and many of my Methodist brethren came
back and took possession of their tents, which
they had left in my care. This I was very glad
of, for I began to have enough to attend to.—
The congregation was so large, that the pedlers
took their old stands again, on the same conditions as before. The next Sunday the people

began to come very early, and kept coming un-til the whole tent was filled, and came till the whole circle of tents was full, and the whole grove literally filled with people, while the preaching was listened to with great attention. I could not hear much of it, for as the congre-gation was large, and some rowdyism began to appear, it took my attention mostly; but I was pretty well prepared if the "Cainites" did not behave, for we had the high sheriff and one of his deputies (Adams), and R. A. Chapman, attorney, was present, and would attend to them at short notice, and did to some of them. But very good order prevailed, and the meeting in-creased in interest, together with its vast num-bers. The first time Bro. Himes attempted to call on sinners to come forward to the altar for prayers, I truly thought him beside himself, for our meeting had been crowned with such success that I did not think any would come for-ward, and I kept watch while the three first verses were being sung, when there was such a rush to the altar for prayers as I had never seen. This gave *me* the "lock-jaw" for awhile, for I was so astonished to see those forward who had stood through our meeting, that I did not speak for sometime : truly, I thought, God was in the place and I knew it not : and when prayer was offered, such a work ensued as had not been seen on that ground before. Some of my friends were forward, and *some* church members—all

pleading for mercy : it was a noisy place indeed.
Our officers came to me and said, " This is
worse than the Methodist prayer-circle." I
suppose they meant as to noise. I recollect
asking Bro. Hawks what he thought of it. He
answered, " It is the work of God in good earnest." By this time a number had come out
happy, and were rejoicing, which carried the
evidence to us, that if *ours* was the work of God,
that must be. Bro. Hawks went into the work
as usual, laboring for sinners, while prejudice
was giving way before the work of God. This
meeting continued through with power, and was
instrumental in more conversions than the other,
saying nothing of the truth that was received
by thousands at this meeting. *I* did not receive
the doctrine, for I had not time to examine it,
nor did I want to. Immediately after the meeting, I was shown a piece in a Baptist paper,
published in Hartford, stating that the Millerite meeting at our place was a money-making
affair, and that Himes had got a great amount
of money, and I think it stated nearly a barrel
of jewelry : at any rate, it was all a *great lie*,
whether it was meant for one or not, and I knew
it, and felt it duty to give all the facts of the
case, and did so, and it was published in the
" Signs of the Times." This was the first time
I had ever written for publication. I should
not have written then, only I had all the minutes of *expense* of both meetings, to a cent, and

all that was *collected*, and knew what the "*jew-elry*" was prized at and *sold for* ; and I felt it duty to speak out in defence of one who had been so maliciously belied. At this meeting, one or two circumstances took place, perhaps worthy of a remark. One night, at 11 o'clock, two great rowdies came on to the ground, and refused to go off when requested by the night-watch. I was called up, and took Bro. Tilden, and went to see them. They refused to go until they got ready. I told them that this was a "time meeting," and it was *time* for them to be going, and I would give them one minute to start in, and then, if they did not go, I would find lodging for them. The smallest one started ; he was acquainted with me ; his name was White. The other threatened some, told what he *had* done, and what he *would* do. When the time was up, I ventured to take hold of him. Bro. Tilden and I took him to the stand, where he was bound, and delivered over to " Cæsar," and had the honor and profit of it, the latter of which was about $10 out of his pocket. Another evening, three men came on to the ground, they *said*, on purpose to fight with me. The watch tried to get them off, but it was no use ; they were bent upon making trouble. I was in bed, and I *think* it was Bro. Ladd who came and called me, and told me what was going on, and that I must get up and do something. I went out, and at first thought that I would

put them all into the stand ; but observing that
the one who wanted to fight with me, had the
marks of a gentleman, when sober, I had a disposition to take hold of him, and told him that
I never had fought since I was a boy, but if he
would own whipped, if I could handle him at
wrestling, *I* would do the same. His comrades
said that was fair, and he agreed to it. We
went back into the woods. Bro. Ladd or
Stebbins was there. We took hold, and I calculated to handle him hard, and I guess *he*
thought so, for he cried, *"fairly done,"* a number of times. I kept him moving until he was
satisfied he was much better off than he would
have been to have fought, as he first proposed.
I pitied the fool, and took him to my tent, and
he slept with *me* that night, and his comrades
in another tent, but they left as soon as day appeared, leaving *him* with *me*. He slept until
breakfast was ready. I called him up, and
made him sit with me at the head of the table,
and if ever a fellow looked cheap, *he* did. He
told me that he had not a well bone in him,
and that he never was so sore in all his life,—
probably he told the truth. This had a better
effect than prosecuting would. He lives within
four miles of me, and is worth a great deal of
property, but he has not wanted to fight with
me since then.

The next week after this meeting closed, Bro.
L. C. Collins offered me $25 to go to Plainville,

and take charge of another Advent camp-meeting, which I accepted. I took (of a Mr. Richards) a lease of one hundred rods, each way, from the centre of the ground. At this meeting a great many attended who were at the other meeting ; although it was over fifty miles, Bro. George Storrs was there, and other Advent preachers. I had more time, here, to examine their doctrine, and I was astonished, when I read the Bible for myself, without a Papal comment upon it. I was convinced that they had got the truth on the *nature of the events,* saying nothing of the *time,* and many things I learned that I never knew were in the Bible before. It was a new book indeed, and had some promises that I never had thought belonged to us. In fact I had never read expecting to understand for myself, and thousands are in the same situation, not even able to give the reason for the hope that is within them.— Nearly all the blindness that there is in the land is in consequence of not searching the Scriptures, as is commanded by Christ, John v : 39, and other places. I do not care if we never get a correct clue to the *time,* the *doctrines* will *stand the test,* and the *practice of them* will give us a " part in the first resurrection, on such the second death will not have power ;" and seeing such new beauty and glory to be revealed at the revelation of Jesus Christ for us, we are commanded to "hasten unto" it, and because we have done so, it is considered a crime, by many, because it did not come ; well, it is *coming* notwithstanding, and those who love it will be ready, and those who hate it will not. This is all true, but as this book is not designed for the discussion of any peculiar views, I proceed with the meeting. Much good was done at this meeting aside from the doctrine ; for many were converted and reclaimed from a backslidden state. Here, rowdyism was plenty, and I well earned my $25. I will relate one circumstance that may interest some who were not there : The latter part of the meeting the "Cainites" became very bold, because (on Bro. Storrs' account) the laws were. not enforced, for he was on the principle of *non-resistance.* Thursday evening, (I think) a lot of the "Cainites" tore down the tent of the colored people, and did other mischief, and then got into their omnibus, and commenced singing obscene songs, and ran their horses so that we could not catch them. The next day, the same team came back with seventeen, and *some* of them came to disturb the meeting, for they were the same that came the day before. I kept thinking how to take them if they commenced their deviltry again. Along towards night, things looked squally, and I was determined that they should not get off my ground without being taken. The land ran one hundred rods each way. I looked at my lease to be sure that it was correct. The road which they took, *to* and *from* the ground, was not a public highway. I selected eight or ten good men, placed them about fifty rods from the camp-ground, with the directions in case they made disturbance to seize the horses on leaving, when I gave the sign, and that was— "catch them." After these were in their places, I selected as many more to stay on the camp-ground *till they started.* Bro. Hawks and Geo. Miller were among them ; and some of the colored brethren. I cut up a clothes-line, for a particular purpose, and gave each man a good string, expecting that the "Cainites" would do as they did the night before, and I was not disappointed. They tore a tent down and then ran for the team, which was all ready to start, and piled in, any how, and the four horses were in a keen run, at the crack of the whip, and we followed as near as possible, they all the while asking, " Won't you ride ? won't you ride ? jump in," &c. When they got to the right place I shouted, " *take them !*" and the boys in ambush appeared, to their astonishment stopped the horses, and we came up ; I told them " yes, I *will* ride *now*," and, getting into the omnibus commenced pitching them out over the sides on the ground, while the brethren secured them. The 'strings' were very handy and were used to good advantage. While I was at work pitching them out, Bro. George Miller discovered a sword or dirk drawing out

of a cane, and cried, "Look out for that dirk."
I looked round and saw the man that had it,
and taking him by the collar and the seat of his
pants, he went overboard so quick, that he only
had time to say '*O, dear,*' before *he*, dirk and
all, after an aerial journey of some twenty feet
landed on the ground some feet from the wagon,
and Bro. Miller took good care of him, until we
got the whole load secured. There was one, a
miller by trade, or disguised in miller's clothes ;
he was stout and stubborn, and was determined
not to be bound. My nerves were strung up
pretty high by this time, seeing their conduct,
and the dirk. I made haste to secure him—I
felt that I could handle him, and laid him on
the ground so roughly that he begged, and said
that I had broken his back, and some of the
brethren thought I had better 'let him up.'
He took on so bitterly with his *broken back*,
that he got the sympathy of some, and he was
not bound. But as soon as he got a chance he
started upon a keen run for the woods. One
of the colored men whose name was Fuller,
bounded after him like a deer, and in a moment
caught him, before reaching the woods, and
brought him back, puffing and blowing, exclaim-
ing, "here is your man with a broken back,"
and we bound him with the rest. They were
all taken back to the ground, except the driver,
whom I let go, he having made good promises
not to be caught in another such mean scrape.

I took his name, and he was glad to be off.
After a while, a consultation was held to know
what was to be done with the prisoners. Some
thought one thing, and some another; most
however, thought it would be right to proceed
with them according to law, and that immediately. But I saw a difficulty in that, as there
was not a Justice of the peace in that vicinity,
and it was now nearly twelve o'clock, Saturday
night, and as we *had them,* I proposed taking
their names, having a season of *prayer,* and,
unbinding them, letting them go. But some
were opposed to this, for they said that they
deserved punishment, and I thought that Bro.
Storrs' *non-resistance* began to fail him, as he
was at first opposed to letting them off so easily.
But I saw an objection, and reasoned with them
thus: We cannot keep them until Monday, if
we would. The sound had gone abroad, and
if we kept them bound, all the rowdies in that
region would be out, next day, and break up
the meeting in spite of all we could do, and we
should fail in our object, and punish ourselves
worse than we did them. Finally the brethren
concluded my way was best, especially Bro.
Storrs. I went to the tent, and talked with
the prisoners, telling them what I had concluded
to do if they would give their names, which they
glady did, confessed their folly, and were sorry.
Before unbinding them I told them that we
should have a season of prayer, and wished them

to stay, which they did, and a part of them
wept, and kneeled down with us. They confessed more after prayers, especially the one
who drew the dirk. He came from Hartford
that day, and begged of us not to prosecute him.
It would be a great crime to draw a dirk under
those circumstances, and it would kill his mother.
Others confessed, and all commended our *courage* in our own defence, and especially the *mercy* that we had shown them. One man said,
"I am the captain of a military company in
Hartford, and no money would have tempted
me to come if I had thought that the *rest*, or
some of them would have acted so ; but as I am
in the scrape, I shall have to stand it. I have
got to be at the head of my company on parade
Monday morning at sunrise, and now I am a
prisoner. The others knew that he tried to
keep order, and they admitted that he did, and
if they had heard to him, this would not have
happened. One of the men was a merchant in
Hartford—he said, "I had rather be kicked to
pieces, only leave my head whole, so that my
wife will know me, than to be kept bound until
daylight." After a long chat, we took the dirk
cane, and cut off fifteen inches of the blade as
evidence against them if we saw fit to prosecute
them. After the meeting closed, they all saw
their situation if we did proceed against them.
All were as guilty as the one who drew the dirk,
but I gave the cane to the man, showing him

what I had cut off, leaving enough sc that it did not spoil the cane. We then took off the cords and set them at liberty, hoping that this would work for their good, for which they thanked us, and left us docile as lambs. How they got home, twelve or fifteen miles, I do not know, for their horses had been gone some hours, and were probably at home. We had no more disturbance from that source or company. We did not prosecute them, and the last that I heard of any of them, two had died, and the one who had the dirk, I have understood, gave good evidence of conversion to Christianity before he died. As many have heard of this affair, and had not probably got the facts, I think it worth relating, as this work is designed to give a correct statement of all these skirmishes, at the camp-meetings with which I was identified. The above was witnessed by many others, whose names I have forgotten.

I do not consider the above an act of *grace*, neither have I felt condemned for bringing the guilty to *justice*. I always have made it a rule to show mercy after I get the victory over an enemy. I attended other meetings that fall, but did not have the charge of them, and therefore had but little to do with the "Cainites;" nothing worth relating that I distinctly recollect. There are many interesting circumstances that I have partly forgotten, that I shall not mention.

I shall only take a few, and such as I can recollect distinctly, and can prove by living witnesses if questioned.   In 1843-4, I attended meetings all of the time, either camp or protracted meetings ; for the work of reformation spread in all directions.   I remember of going to Middletown to labor with Bro. Hawks and K. S. Hastings, and there was a powerful work.   It lasted for months in spite of all opposition from a lukewarm church and the "Cainites" combined, which is always the way when God works.   Recollect, the Roman soldiers were willing to serve the church, when the church said that Christ was heterodox, and the "Cainites" ran the risk of their lives by telling a lie to please a backslidden church, by saying that the disciples stole Christ away while *they*, the Roman soldiers, committed a capital offence by getting asleep. But the church agreed to back them up in this lie, if they would stick to it.   I could relate facts and *prove them*, showing that church-members have done no better than this, in these few years of my experience in the doctrine of the Advent near.   The devil hates this the worst of anything that I have seen yet.   He knows his time is short, and the shorter the better.

I remember attending a protracted meeting in Westminster in company with Bro. Levi Allen, where the "Cain family" attempted to break up our meeting.   They tried *every* way that they could think of ; at last, they got into the upper part of the town hall with a band of music over where our meeting was being held. But, in spite of them, we got a number forward for prayers. The work of God could not be *drummed* out of the place, and they said there was no use, for the brethren would pray louder than they could drum, or something like it. I remember one evening when the rabble again undertook to break up the meeting by throwing chestnuts, talking, &c. The preacher was broken off in his sermon, and I got up and exhorted the people of God to keep looking to Him for help. Bro. Allen arose and commenced ; he soon got to crying for God to " work among the wicked," and there was such a power in it that the wicked all started, and the door was crowded to see which would get out first. I do not believe if a wild tiger had been let loose among them, they would have cleared the house any quicker. The work went on, and they dare not come in again until the meeting closed, and *then* only a few dare venture, for they never saw it in that fashion before. " Call this religion ?" said one, as he returned after meeting to get his hat—" Frighten a man to death." Sure enough, they were frightened, but we had peace. We got the victory and left. On our way home we stopped at. a friend of Bro. Allen for a short time. I got home-sick, as they were all strangers to me, and wanted to go home that night, but to accommodate him, I consented to stay.

There were no Advent meetings in the place, nor any other that evening. While Bro. Allen was out in the fields with his friend, I sat in the house reading. There was a young and intelligent looking woman getting supper. I thought of asking her if she enjoyed religion ; but knowing that I was going away in the morning, and she being an entire stranger and so busy, I deferred it for that time. Soon after I felt it a duty to ask her, which I did. She answered me, " No, sir !" I replied, " You are too good looking for the devil to have." This was all that was said. I then went out where Bros. Allen and Barrows were looking at some fat cattle : they called my attention to them, but I took no interest in them. It appeared to me that God would get hold of that woman in the house, and I said so, which seemed to astonish Barrows, for said he, " She has had more prayers offered for her, than for any other person I know of." She had lived through a great reformation in that place, and nothing had moved her yet, and all the preachers that came there, felt interested in her case, especially Bro. Cook, the Baptist minister of that place. Barrows wanted to know what made me think that the Lord was at work with her. I told him I did not *know*, but it seemed so to me. He replied, "I hope your impressions are correct," and he went off about his business, and I went off by myself. Nothing was said during supper

time upon the subject. Bros. Allen and Barrows and his wife had a good time visiting, and
talking over old times ; but as I never had seen
them before, I took no interest in their conversation. I wanted the time to come for family
prayers, for I wanted to *pray*. When the time
came, Bro. Allen was asked to lead, he being
an old friend. This young woman sat in her
chair, and I told her, if she would kneel down,
I would pray for her. After some hesitation,
she dropped upon her knees to the astonishment
of all present, especially her mother, who was
gone from home when we arrived. I had great
liberty in praying for her, and after I had finished, they all prayed around again for her.—
This routed the rest in the house and some of
the neighbors, for while we were praying, Bro.
Cook, the Baptist minister, and his wife, heard
strange voices in prayer after they were in bed,
and seeing a light down at Bro. Barrows, got up,
partly dressed themselves, and came in while I
was praying the second time. I shall always
recollect his first words, as he entered the house :
" Glory to God !" He and his wife took hold
with us, and all worked in harmony. But it
did not affect her any, and I felt it duty to ask
her to pray for herself, which she did, but her
prayer was very short. All prayed around again,
but still without any effect. I asked her if she
was willing to make any sacrifice for God : she
said she was, and would do anything to get re-

lief, for her conviction was strong; but all the spirit of supplication seemed to cease at once. I thought *something* was the matter, I asked her if she had given up all. She said she could not think of anything else, but wanted *I* should pray again, for she could not live so. I then discovered the wedge of gold. She had on *jewelry,* and I proposed to her to take it off, and make it a sacrifice to God. She did not comply, but kept upon her knees. Bro. Cook and his wife prayed again, but no change. I then told her I believed God would convert her that night if she would make up her mind to take off those little "gods of gold," and that I could not pray for her again until she did. Bro. Cook said that he thought this was going too far; for God did not look at the gold, but the heart. But I insisted upon it, and all at once she began taking it off, and putting it upon the chair; and when the last piece was off, God took her in hand, and, instead of *my* praying, *she* occupied the time in good earnest, and in a few moments was converted, and came out very clear and happy. We all rejoiced, especially Bro. Barrows, and Bro. Cook and his wife, for they had labored so much and so long for her conversion, that they were discouraged. While we were all rejoicing, down came a doctor and his wife from up stairs, and wanted prayers. It appears that God's Spirit had ransacked the house. I did not know of any one else living in the house.

but late as it was, Bro. Cook and his wife stayed, and we all prayed for the doctor. His exercise of mind and body was so great that he sweat like a man mowing. I think the doctor and his wife *both* got converted that night. This I believe was Friday night, and Saturday morning we expected to ,go home. The young people came in to see Miss Barrows at an early hour. She had not slept off her religion, and told with great boldness what God had done for her the evening before, and it cut like a new two-edged sword, for she had been so very hard, and had stood in the way of the work of the Lord so long, that it surprised all of the village, and when they *heard* that she was converted, they wanted to see for themselves and be sure, especially her young associates. As they came in, she exhorted them, telling them how good religion was.— These truths were backed up by the Spirit of God, and conviction was all over the place. Instead of our taking the cars for home that morning, as we expected, we stayed, for sinners were enquiring what they must do to be saved. We commenced praying and laboring for them in our weak way, and God blessed many, and we kept up meetings all the next day and evening and until a late hour Saturday night, and at every meeting more or less were converted.— Sunday morning I thought that sectarianism was at work, and I persuaded Bro. Allen to join me and get a team, to go ten or twelve

miles to a *Methodist* quarterly meeting. We got
the team and started early, and when we were
about to start, some one told us that we were
not in the way of duty, and that we were running away from the work of God which we had
started, and that there were going to be some
baptized that morning, and that we had better
stay ; but it was all to no purpose, for I had determined not to stay there any longer—so we
started. Soon the *harness* gave way ; but we
repaired it, and went on awhile longer, and then
the wagon broke down and run us into a ditch
or a fence. This time Bro. Allen spoke about
what we were told before we started, of running
away from duty, but I remember how I, in my
sectarian Methodism felt and perhaps said, that
I would not stay there and attend the *Baptist*
meeting, for we should not hear anything that
would profit us, for they were going to baptise
some that morning who were only a day old, &c.,
so we drove on to the meeting, and it was
" death in the pot." I was disappointed and
more home-sick than before, and we started back
before the last meeting, and found that we had
lost a great deal by going away, for in the morning while Bro. Cook was baptizing, the power
of God settled down upon the congregation, and
some were " slain" under it, and sinners were
still enquiring. We got back in the afternoon
and went to work for them again in the old
kitchen of Bro. Barrow, God working in power

until evening, when Bro. Cook came in and said that there were hundreds out of doors, and he wished the meeting to be removed over to the Baptist church, a few rods from there, and he was so anxious that I told the people that they had better go over, and then closed the meeting. All but a few went. I then thought as he had got the meeting on his hands, I should do no more about it, and did not go over.

Here I hesitate about giving the rest of the account, for it will look to some, as if I was taking too much honor upon myself, which God knows is not the case, for I never had a worse trial in all my life up to that time, than I had for a short time, after the people had gone over to the meeting house. I felt like this, and I mean to speak the truth in the fear of God in this thing, if it goes against MY feelings. I felt as though it was all a contrived plan to break up our meeting in the kitchen of Bro. Barrows, where God began to work, and get it over to the Baptist church for a sectarian purpose, and I would not go near it, and I did not believe that God would work over there, especially if this was the case, and many things ran through my mind of a jealous nature, while in this trial of an hour or so. About 8 o'clock, some one came over, to have me go over to the meeting house, for there were a great many in, and the meeting was dead ; nothing had moved. I would not go, for I thought, that they might work it

out themselves. They came again, and I made
some excuses, but at last consented to go, but
would not take any part in the exercises. When
I got there, the house was a perfect jam ; the
galleries and all the aisles were full. I stood
in one aisle, and saw Bro. Allen in another, on
the other side of the church near the pulpit.
I tried to beckon to him to go out, but Bro.
Cook called on him to go forward, which he did,
and then called on me, but I did not go. A man
whom I supposed to be the deacon, came to me,
and requested me to go with him to the altar.
Every eye was upon us, and I felt like death,
for I had said that I *would not* take any part
in the exercises in the *Baptist Church*. But
he was so urgent, that I went and took a seat
with him near the altar, and there was an effort
made to get sinners forward for prayers, but not
one came. Bro. Cook told me that it was my
duty to take hold, for he could not do anything
as long as we were present. His wife said something to that effect in my presence. I thought
of going out, but Bro. Allen was on the other
side of the house, and I was at a loss whether
to break my promise, and do what little I could,
or run. I was not used to such straight places
as this. Here I was among strangers, in a Baptist meeting house, crowded full, the preacher,
his wife, and the deacon, present, and all in-
sisting on my doing something, and it did seem
for a few minutes as if they looked to *man*,

more than to God, and a very weak man, too, for I shook and trembled like a leaf. I finally told Bro. Cook that I couldn't stand it so, but didn't want to move, for my way was so different from other people's that some would be astonished, and, perhaps, leave the house. To this he replied, " Take your own course ; the burden of the meeting is on you." I was then on my feet ; I recollect of standing a short time, until my trembling stopped. Perfect silence prevailed by this time. I recollect distinctly the first words I spoke, and nearly all I said for a few moments, for it seemed as if an invisible dictator was helping me. The words were as follows : " Three good unimpeachable witnesses were sufficient to cause any man in the congregation to be hung by the neck, until he was *dead*, DEAD, DEAD. if he was guilty, and, as every sinner was guilty, and under sentence of death, they must die unless a Mediator was applied for, who was willing and able to save all who applied." I then introduced Christ as the one who was willing and able, and had shown himself so, within two or three days. I was going to call on the witnesses to testify to this fact, and I should get more than *three*, and every one that arose would be a swift witness against every sinner in the house. I then called on those who had been converted or blessed within two or three days to arise. Miss Barrows rose first, and then others followed in exhorta-

tion which had a good effect. Bro. Cock and
his wife shouted for joy, for they saw that the
work of God was going on. I next requested
the front seat to be cleared for the converts, that
they might be together, which was done. I
then requested the second seat to be vacated.
By this time I had forgotten that it was a Baptist meeting, and called on sinners to come forward if they wanted the prayers of God's people, and of those young converts. They came
immediately and filled the second seat, and the
third one was vacated and that was filled. I
then wanted the fourth vacated, and when *that*
was done, I saw a wonderment pictured on many
countenances, to know what the last seat stood
empty for. I then called upon the old hopers
that had not done anything for sinners for
months, to come forward, and go to work in
God's cause, and show those, then forward, that
they were interested in their case. In a few
minutes the seats were filled, and I think that
two of them were filled with members of the
church. A prayer meeting commenced in good
earnest. I do not remember many particulars
after this, for it was one continual scene of praying and shouting for some time. A number
got blessed, and the wicked looked God-forsaken,
especially those in the galleries, who were looking down on their young companions who had
taken a step so much wiser than they had by
staying back. When the meeting broke up,

some went over to Bro. Barrows' house, and
we prayed for them till very late, for we were
going away in the morning train at an early hour.
Some others came in and wanted us to pray for
them before we went. We spent the time in
praying until we heard the whistle of the engine,
and then left very suddenly. I heard afterwards
that some came out clear that morning after we
left. There are many who will remember Bro.
Barrows' kitchen in Jewett city.

I did not think of penning so many of these
circumstances when I commenced to write a
sketch of my life ; but some friends thought it
worth while, and I conform to their wishes. I
write entirely from memory, and cannot hope to
be exact in language ; but I find, come to take
things up, my memory improves very much, so
that events of years ago seem but yesterday to
me while writing. I have consulted a number
of persons who are referred to in this narrative,
and find that I have got circumstances correct
thus far. After we got home from this tour of
nearly two weeks, and attended to our business
matters, we started again on a similar errand to
try to work for the good of others. We stopped
in Hartford, Conn. We had a number of good
meetings, and some in the house where we boarded. The Bro. and his wife had just been converted, and their hearts were warm and full of
zeal. Thinking no evil, they of course supposed
that their friends, being professors, would love

every one that loved God and was trying to serve
Him. They gave us an introduction to their
friends and boarders at the supper table. All
passed off quietly for that time. In the evening, after meeting, we returned, had a praying
season, which stirred the elements of sectarianism from the bottom. Poor children, they little
thought what trouble it would make them by
asking us home with them. The next morning
we ate breakfast *alone ;* not a boarder or rela-
tive, who were there the day before, were at
the table. I saw that something was 'to pay,'
and tried to find out the cause. I thought of
leaving. Bro. Allén *did* go over to Mansfield,
some twenty miles, to see his friends, and I was
alone, pondering over these things. I saw the
good brother and his wife crying and looking
very sad ; there was some talking, which led me
to believe that our coming there had made a
fuss in the family, and I ate my supper at another place. As there was an appointment out
for that evening, I concluded to stay to the
meeting, and then leave, and either go home,
or over where brother Allen had gone. But
the meeting was very good, and when it was
time to close, I felt like giving an invitation for
any one to come forward for prayers who felt
the need of them. One man came (a stranger
to me), and I think a number of others came.
We had a season of prayer, and this man in
particular felt very deeply, and I prayed the

second time, and gave him the best advice that
I could, and began to look up another lodging
place for that night, calculating to leave in the
morniĥg, for I saw plainly that the devil was
'in the wind' up on Main-street, where I had
been staying with brother Allen. He had gone,
and I would not stay in that place and work
alone, for I depended much upon him, as he
was the instrument of getting me to believe that
I could do anything, often telling me that if I
would try to do it, God would help me, &c. I
for years found fault with *him* and *others* for
not conducting meetings right, and would not
take any part myself on the account of incom-
petency, bashfulness, and other trivial excuses.
These did not satisfy him, until I ventured to
make the trial. I never shall forget the first
time that I ever undertook to open a meeting.
Others will recollect it too. It was only the
year before this, in 1843. But to return.—
While I was talking about going home with
some one, this man who was forward for prayers
gave me an invitation to go home with him, for
he wanted to talk with me. I accepted the invitation, and, to my astonishment, went to the
very house where I first went, and where I supposed the devil was raised, and had quit. Here
I found the Bro. and his wife before alluded to,
crying, and what it meant I did not know : it
seemed to be mingled with joy and thankfulness.
Nothing was said that I remember, and we went

to bed in the very chamber where Bro. Allen
and I stayed before. He wished me to pray for
him before going to bed, as he had not got rid
of his burden, which I did, and then told him
to pray for himself, which he did ; and he felt
better. After we got in bed, he wanted to know
how I came there, what my profession was, and
what I did for a living, &c. I told him that I
was a miller by trade, and a Millerite by profession, and had come down with Bro. Levi
Allen to hold a few meetings : *he* had gone, and
I was going in the morning : but he seemed to
doubt it. I was a little inclined to be *skittish*,
but thinking a man that prayed as he did, could
not be a dangerous one, I dismissed those feelings. Soon he commenced telling me how *he*
came there, and it was as follows : He had that
day received a letter from one of his brother's
boarders, a friend, stating that John had got
two Millerites there, and they could not sleep
nights, &c. and as he (this man) owned the
property, the boarders notified him that they
had quit boarding with John, his brother, and
should not eat again at his table, until he came
down and made John rout us or did it himself ;
and he came for that purpose, and tried to have
John tell me to go, for he had learned that the
other one had gone. John, not knowing that I
had made up my mind to go, told him, Daniel,
that he could not and *would not* turn his brethren out of the house, if he had to beg his bread.

He might do the errand himself. After a long talk. John cried and felt so bad, that it set the family affections at work, and Daniel wanted to know what to do. I think he said that John told him that if he would go to meeting that evening, he would see whether it were himself or his boarders that were to blame in making such a fuss. He told me that John got him to promise that he would go, and that was the reason why he was there, and he thanked God that he went and began to rejoice. By this time I began to see the hand of God in this work. I could then account for John and his wife feeling so badly the day before, and their strange crying just before we went to our chamber. His brother Daniel, who had been sent for to turn me out of the house, had been forward for prayers, and had invited me home with him, and of course had taken all the responsibility off of *them*, he being the owner of the property. I could not sleep much, for I kept thinking, wondering, and wishing that Bro. Allen was there. In the morning, while they were getting breakfast, Daniel was out, I suppose among his friends telling what God had done for him. When the time came for prayers, I saw the folding doors open, and *another family* in the other part of the room. This was the first I knew of it, and an old and venerable looking man came up to me and asked me to go in the other room, and I discovered some faces there that I saw at the table the first time that Bro. Allen and I took supper there. The old gentleman asked my forgiveness. I could not forgive him, for I had never seen him before, as I knew of, and what this all meant, I did not know. But he said that God had been there, and he knew it not, and that he was among the rest that sent for Daniel to turn us away, and God had done a work for Daniel which put him thinking, and he could not rest until he made a confession.— He was a Baptist deacon. After telling this strange tale, he asked me to pray, but I could not ; for this affair was clothed with such a mystery, I could cry, but could not pray, nor could any one else. There was a general crying time for some minutes. In a short time the deacon prayed, and when he got through I tried, but could not help mixing crying and praying together, whether it was popular or not. I felt that God was at work, and I did not care how the Spirit did work. All that professed religion prayed, and I discovered one in the farther part of the room crying, and felt it a duty to go and ask her if she wanted to serve the Lord. She said she did. We had a season of prayer for her, and she was blessed. Her face fairly shone with the joy that she felt.— This family prayer meeting lasted until nine o'clock in the morning. Those present will re- member this time—*I* shall never forget it. The brother-in-law of John and Daniel, one of the

petitioners for my removal, saw the old deacon
and others break down, and found that *he* had
" a case in court," too, and went out to *the
barn* to get rid of it. But God was going to
work in his own way, and brought him *in again*.
He wanted prayers, and got them, and God
blessed him. He then got his daughter forward,
and *she* was blessed. He then got a team, and
went about twelve miles after his *wife*, and she
was blessed : so the whole family went home rejoicing in God. The last time I saw them they
were holding on. The work seemed thoroughly
done. How many days I stayed after Daniel
was converted I do not recollect ; but I did not
get turned out of the house. The deacon's son-
in-law often inquired how we obtained a living.
I told him, by working with our hands, and he
gave us $25 each. and told us to spend it in the
work of home missionaries, for he had made up
his mind that he had paid enough to foreign
missions, and he had concluded to pay us $100,
$25 each at a time, to keep at this work until
it was gone, and when the $50 was gone, to call
for $50 more. Soon after this, Daniel sent me
a letter desiring me to come to T——, twelve
miles from Hartford, where he owned a tavern,
and hold some meetings. His brother John
came after us, and myself and wife, Bro. Hawks
and Bro. Allen, started and got there about
noon. But Daniel was disappointed in getting
a house, so he had a meeting in the dining-room

at his tavern in the afternoon. The Lord began to work in the first meeting, and before it closed, the bar-keeper and others were on their knees for prayers. This was a strange thing for a tavern. When their customers came in and inquired for the bar-keeper, they found him in another room, forward for prayers,—and this strange and sudden overturn ran like fire in dry stubble. The neighbors came in, and among them one or two preachers. When they saw that God was at work, they offered Daniel their meeting houses, which they denied him before. If I recollect rightly, the Baptists opened their church *first*, and brother Hawks preached from Daniel v : 27, and God commenced his work on the spot, for while he was preaching, my wife, for the first time, I think, had a peculiar exercise. She lost her strength, and stood upon her feet some time, perfectly paralyzed and stiff.— This was a strange thing to me at that time, but a good old "mother in Israel," known as mother Bryant, was present, and said it was the work of God, and I did not try to hinder it, for I had much confidence in her judgment in religious matters. After the meeting was closed or preaching done, a number were convinced of sin by seeing this strange exercise. The next evening there was no need of ringing the bell, for it had been rung the night before, and to some purpose, for the house was *full* at an early hour. The Lord's work went on in both churches,

for we went first to the Baptist and then to the
Methodist, and so on for nearly a week, and the
whole place was moved. Some Catholics were
forward for prayers. When we had a notice of
a conference in our place, we came home very
suddenly, and left the meeting with the two
preachers.

I recollect when we got into the meeting-
house at home, Moses Stoddard came to me,
and said we had run away from our work down
there, and from God, and ought to go back.—
He offered to go back with us, but we did not,
and sure enough there the work has stopped by
trying to *proselyte*.

We stayed at home a while, and I will state
some of the circumstances which happened in
our own village at different times. Some took
place before the above and some after, but all in
the village where I now live. Others will recollect the facts when they see them. As I have
always had more or less to do with the " Cain
family," here some things may be of interest to
others, that *I* never thought of laying up, much
less of publishing. One Sabbath, I arrived at
meeting rather late, and the meeting had not
begun. The people were standing outside of the
house. It appears that a crazy man had got
into the church, taken a seat, and began talking
and swearing, and the minister, Bro. Bosworth,
told the people that he should not begin the
meeting until the man was removed, and a num-

ber of efforts were made to get him out, but he
resisted. When I came up, there was a revelation of the fact, and I went in and tried to flat-
ter him out, but all to no purpose. I informed
the congregation that he *would* go out, and they
must be quiet for a few moments. I took hold
of him, and started ; he took hold of a seat, and
kept hold. But I was enabled to carry him out.
Some screamed, but he was soon at the door,
and when he saw that he had got to go out, he
tried to bite my hand. I let go of him, and he
went out headlong, and hurt him a very little.
Why I name this, is because some at the time
not knowing the facts of the circumstance, found
fault with the act, and thought no one ought to
be ejected from the house of God. I do not record this as an act of *grace,* nor a *privilege,* but
a *duty.* He never was seen there again, although
he lived in the place for years.

Another duty presented itself about this time.
On coming home one day, I heard that one of
our neighbors was dead, and I was sent for, to go
and help lay him out. I thought strange, for
there were enough near by ; the boy that came
after me, said that there were four there already.
When I arrived, nothing had been done. It
was a bad job, and the four agreed that if I
would get a kettle and heat some water, they
would do the rest. I was glad of this chance,
and went into the kitchen to the old lady, (or
devil) for a kettle. She refused, and flew into

a rage. I saw then why nothing had been done, and I had got the worst job after all! They told me that she would not let *them* have a thing, and this was the *wife* of the deceased. This was so inhuman, that I determined to fulfill *my* contract, and went to look for a kettle. I found one at the back of the house, and took hold of it, and as I stooped over, the old hag jumped on my back, evidently with the intention to break me down, for she weighed over 200 pounds, some thought 300 ; but, as I had agreed to do that part of the work, I went at work to do it, and I carried the kettle, old woman and all into the house. This created such a laugh that it did not look or appear much like the house of death. After she got into the house, she went to the door after the kettle, for the men had taken it into the room where the corpse was, and in spite of four good strong men who were holding the *door*, she got it part way open. I took hold of her to pull her back, but could not reach around her, and she had got part way into the room again, but, among us all, we got the door closed. She insisted upon getting the kettle. I thought if I had got to do any more, I would do something in earnest. I took hold of her clothes, put my foot against the ceiling and laid out my strength to pull her away from the door, when the door handle came off, and we both landed across the kitchen and fell on the floor, and it fell to my lot to keep her there,

until her husband was "laid out." She abused
him in his last sickness, which the people thought
shortened his days. This *disagreeable duty*,
SHE never forgot, while she lived, and *I* never
shall. The men present, were Davis Dunham,
Theodore Williams, Seth Clough, Thos. Frost,
and Jacob Yance. They are all but one living,
and in this place, and will recollect this dis-
graceful scene, and another about the same
time, with a demon in human shape, who drove
his family off to his neighbors, and I was again
obliged to do another duty, more disagreeable
than the above, but I will not relate it. The
"Cain family" do not like me because I have
always taken up against them, and have been
very lucky in bringing them to justice, some
way or other, sooner or later, and it is a proverb
among many, that "OLD MUNGER will find you
out." I have made myself ridiculous, by contending for the right way in this ungodly world
through which I am now passing. I have had
to do with thieves, robbers, Sabbath-breakers,
rowdies, rummies, and murderers more or less,
for many years in this place. There are such a
number of curious circumstances connected with
my life, that I shall omit most of them where
they are not connected with religious meetings.
I have learned by experience, that when I get
a victory over an enemy or opponent, that it is
an act of mercy to show mercy, as in the case
of the seventeen rowdies who were taken and

bound at the Newington camp-meeting.—— There are hundreds in this vicinity that know I have spared no pains to detect them, and when I have done it, they have been let off in the easiest manner, especially if they were willing to "own up" and yield, and promise to behave. Of all that 1 have entered complaint against, for various crimes, I have never intended to punish them to the extent of the law, and I dare appeal to the whole "Cain family," that I have had to do with in these matters, and let them take a vote, and I will get nearly all to testify to the above assertion.

I now remember a circumstance that occurred here, which I will relate. There was a man by the name of Philips, the first inventor of "friction matches," who got drunk, and abused the citizens beyond measure. One Sunday the tavern keeper, although a sheriff, applied to me for help, and as it was Sunday, and I was tithing man, (which I had been for many years,) he thought it proper to take him for breach of the Sabbath. The next day, I think, he (Philips) came into the village and began as before, threatening and swearing at a great rate, when I put a warrant into the hand of one of Cæsar's household, and he immediately demanded my assistance, to help take him, for he was a dangerous desperado. We gave chase to the wagon. It had three persons in it of the same stamp. We cornered them and stopped the horse, and Philips jumped out near an officer, a Mr. Hubbard, who caught him, and before we could get there, Philips struck Hubbard on the head with a loaded whip stock, and laid him senseless across a low fence, and raised the whip to strike the second blow, which must have proved fatal, just as we arrived. Without thinking, I struck Philips one blow and *he* lay senseless by him, on the same fence, and did not revive until we had carried him nearly a quarter of a mile. They were both in the tavern when the doctor arrived to do up the wound of the officer. He said that Philips looked the worst hurt, and he *did* the *next day*, for I certainly never saw a man so blacked up, even with a dozen blows. He could not see the day he had his trial. I felt that he ought to be considered some on account of his looks ; but it appeared that he was an old offender, and no mercy was shown him, and he paid a heavy fine.— Now it was my turn : he then vented his spite all upon me, and swore revenge ; for I had complained of him and stopped up both his eyes, and he said, that the first time that he saw me after he got well, there would be *another* lawsuit, if not a *funeral*, or something of that kind that made my friends anxious about my safety, and they wished me to keep out of his way — But I didn't want to go skulking through the village, as I had done nothing but my duty under the circumstances. I heard one day that he was in Mr. Barrows' store, threatening me at a great rate ; so I went in, and the storekeeper told him that I had come, and that it was a good time to settle our affairs, and told me what he had just been saying. This was the first time that he had seen me since he had got so he *could* see. He asked me if I was the man who complained of him. I told him I was. He then asked if I struck him, and made him look as he then did. I told him I was the *very man*, and that he had *threatened* enough, and I was ready to have him carry his threats into execution then, and showed some signs of taking hold of him. He said he thought it was a *smaller man* that struck him, and was not ready then ! He soon tamed down, and we talked some time together. I told him how it was—I didn't think of striking him until it was done, and if I hadn't done it, his second blow would have killed Hubbard, the officer, and it was a mercy to him after all, and the rest told him so too. But he was one of Cain's worst boys, and although he dare not put his threats into execution *then*, yet he threatened revenge in some *sly* way. He was going to get help, and secrete himself out near the falls, where I fished every night, and knock me down with a stone or something else, and the water was so swift that it would carry me over the falls. This was told to me, and I was cautioned about going on to the falls one night, for Philips was out there, and had a large man with him. There

had been a rain that day, and the water was
rising. I knew of no other man in town who
dare set a boat out at that pitch of water. He
had waded out before the water rose, and didn't
know his danger, and I *knew* it, and told White,
my comrade, that I was going out on to the falls,
and that if Philips wanted to drown me, he
could do it, for he had threatened enough. We
started, and landed our boat near his. After
making it fast to the anchor placed there for
that purpose by myself, I went up to Philips
and bid him good evening, and told him I had
come to be drowned according to his threats.—
We had each of us a witness, the water was up
just right, and we would settle it very quick.
I gave White my things, hat, bag, &c., and
Philips began to tremble and beg, saying he was
only in fun. I told him that his fun was a serious thing, and I was about to put a stop to it,
by trying who could swim best, &c. He begged, and asked my forgiveness, and would have
got on his knees, but the water was so swift that
he couldn't remain a minute on the falls on his
knees. White and I then went on shore and
turned home. After a few moments I heard a
halloaing, while I was changing my clothes, and
some of the men from the shore came and told
me that the men out on the falls were calling
for me, and had been for some time. I started
and hurried to the spot, about a mile and a half.
When I reached it I couldn't hear what was

said, being down by the water, but I went back
up the bank and could hear distinctly. Philips
was calling my name, and I saw that they had
swamped their boat, and were partly over the
first bar, and would go over the falls unless they
had help soon. Now my courage and mercy
were both tried. Here was my enemy in danger, and as he was subdued, now was the time
to show mercy. I tried to have my comrade go
out again with me to help him, but he refused.
I tried Mr. Murphy and others, and all refused
on account of the danger. The water was still
rising, and they were partly over the first bar,
with their boat full of water, still crying for
help, and calling for me, knowing as all others
did that if any one in town could help them, I
could. Their situation was such that a great
risk must be run to get to them. When no one
else would risk his life to go, I said, " I will try
it alone, if I go over the falls. I will show myself willing to run some risk to save others."—
When I started White got into the boat with
me : I told him what to do. There was a large
rock near where Philips was, and when I got
to that I would tell him and he must jump out
of the bow and hold the boat until I could get
a rope to them, and if we failed, and went over
the falls he must stick to the boat, &c. I saw
that his courage began to fail, and I pushed the
boat into the current, to prevent his getting out,
and so we started. My nerves were like iron.

When I got to the rock, I told him to jump ;
but instead of jumping out of the *bow* of the
boat, as I told him, he jumped out of the side,
and didn't hit the rock, and so he went into the
water out of sight. When he came up, he got
into the boat and wouldn't try it again. But
the cries of the men urged me to try once more,
and I had no one to help, for White was determined not to try it again : I jumped myself and
hit the spot. I held the boat until White got
out, and then we got to them. It was a happy
meeting to *them*, for they were exhausted and
must have given up to the current, very soon.
I ordered them to let their boat go, and get into ours. I succeeded in setting the boat ashore
safely. I should think a hundred people met
us at the water's edge, all rejoicing, and when
we got out we couldn't walk for some time. I
was completely exhausted, but soon got over it.
This was the way that this fuss *ended*, and while
Philips lived he was a good friend to me, often
saying I run the risk of my own life to save his,
and it was so. God delivered him into my hands
to heap coals of fire upon his head. He was shot
two years after in a drunken row, and soon died
of the wound in Cabotville. This is one of many circumstances that I could relate, where it
seems God delivered my enemies up to me to
be merciful to them. I can now think of two
or three such instances ; but I will omit them
for the present, and perhaps wholly, unless they

should be connected with religious meetings.—
To return to the subject of religion in this vicinity, without giving dates, but stating facts.
I had meetings at my house once a week for a
number of years, for the express purpose of
praying for a deeper work of grace in the heart,
or sanctification, as it was called in those days.
I gave out the appointment in this way : There
will be a meeting every Wednesday evening at
my house, for all that love God, and all that
want to love him enough to do their duty.—
This appointment was considered by some as
picking out a certain few, and it created some
sensitiveness in the church, and some nicknamed
the meeting " the upper church," " the picked
party," &c. ; but I felt it my privilege to do as
I *pleased* in my own house, and the fact was
I didn't want *two* classes there. First, there
was a class there that wouldn't do a thing in
meeting, and were only dead lumber. The second class were still worse. They would talk
and pray eternally, and the meeting would run
down all the time. They had nothing but a
form of godliness, and would find fault with
everything that went beyond their narrow contracted views or dead experience. They would
deny or fight the power of the gospel. Paul, in
2 Tim. iii : 5, exhorts Christians to "turn away"
from such as " have the *form* of godliness but
deny the power," and we had obeyed this once
a week at least, and God seemed to be well

pleased ; for if I could remember the number converted and reclaimed at these meetings, the statement would seem incredible in this day of backsliding and formality. With all the scolding and opposition of some of the church, the meetings were well attended by persons of the right stamp. All others kept away, and I was glad of it, for we had to hear their long, dry stuff once or twice a week at the meeting-house, and that was as much as we could bear. At " the upper church," there was scarcely a meeting that there was not some signal manifestation of God's power. I recollect one evening in particular going to bed and leaving eight or ten prostrate in the kitchen. They were shouting and singing all times in the night, until the bell rung in the morning.

These meetings were bad places for sinners to remain in sin. There would occasionally one come in to see what was going on. I have seen many cut down in a moment in answer to prayer. One circumstance I remember in particular. A young man came in, and after we had sung, I told all present the object of the meeting, and if there were any in who did not understand it, and were not willing to kneel down in prayer time, I requested them to retire before we commenced praying, for the meeting was not designed for idlers. Sometimes a number would go out, some muttering about forcing religion upon them. These mostly were members of

the church, and if they had not religion, nor
would show any signs of wanting it by kneel-
ing down, we did not want them there to hinder
the work. These remarks caused some to go
out that evening. But this young man would
not kneel, nor go out unless he was put out.—
The meeting dragged, not much liberty in prayer, for all knew him and his disposition, and I
thought that some of the church members en-
couraged him to take the course that he did ;
for some were ready to do anything to discour-
age us, but I said we would try the strength of
prayer once more, and perhaps God would take
this man in hand, as he had others ; and so it
was, for in less than two minutes he fell on
to the floor, and cried for mercy. This gave the
meeting a new start, and we obtained the victory in spite of the devil that time. I think
others that had gone out came in, and some
came forward for prayers that same evening, for
I recollect distinctly of this young man telling
his friends what God had done for him that
evening, and exhorted them to seek God. He
told what he did before coming to meeting. He
had stolen a *cabbage* coming up to the meeting,
and it was out under my garden fence *then.*—
But God had forgiven him, and he wanted all to
do so. He returned the stolen *cabbage*, and
lived in the enjoyment of religion, and met with
us every meeting. He was not only willing to
kneel, but would *pray* in faith for others, and he

was a great help to the cause of God at that
time. Many will know to whom I refer without
giving his name. He told me that he boarded
with a class-leader at this time, and I know
that *he* was opposed to our meeting, and I had
reason to think that this young man was a tool
for the backslidden or cold part of the church.
But God was with us, and we didn't fear or envy
those who were against us.

Many other circumstances of interest might
be named, that took place in "the upper
church." Some may call this mesmerism, as
skeptics and formalists always have done so, and
rappers do now. Call it what you please ; God
worked, and sinners were converted, and live
their religion out *till this day.* One other case
I will mention. At a Tuesday night meeting
at Bro. Dickinson's, a young·woman came in,
and when the meeting commenced she got up
and told her feelings ; she was in a backslidden
state, but desired to return, and resolved to
serve God better and not quench his Spirit, as
she had done, for that was the cause of her state
of mind, and she was willing to be blessed any
way that God saw fit. In an instant she fell
over backwards with such force that it made the
house jar. Her head struck the floor so heavily
that some were afraid that it had killed her, or
hurt her very badly, for she was stiff, and ap-
parently lifeless. But the meeting went on,
and closed. She remained in the same situa-

tion and position all night, and the next day.
Many came in to see her, and the doctor was
called. Some of the formalists in the church
took every occasion to scoff and put DOWN every
thing that their cold hearts, and small, half
converted heads or minds could not comprehend.
But there were some that had seen hundreds
of such cases, and said that God would bring
her out right, and a doctor would do no good.
They opposed her being moved home, or stirred
until she revived. Wednesday night she lay
just so. Thursday, the formalists determined
to have something done, and proposed giving
her some nourishment, for fear she would starve.
They were told that God would take care of her,
but they got some coffee and fed it to her, but
it didn't work as they expected, and she made
signs for water. After she had drank, she remained in the same quiet state as before, and
in the same place where she fell, all *that* day and
night. Friday morning, there was a stir in the
place, and many came in to see the phenome-
non. I went to Ludlow that day, and told of
it, and I must confess, I was at a loss what to
say, for I had never seen one lie so long before,
and hoped she would revive before I returned
home. But she still lay on the floor. .Some
that were with her that day, said she looked
very happy at times. This was encouraging to
us who had called it the work of the Spirit of
God. There was so much sympathy manifested

for her, both by the formalists and the wicked, because she had lain three days and nights on the hard floor, that we consented to have her moved home to Bro. Ward's house, for she lived with him then. She was removed there, and as it was some distance, we went across the lots, and many were astonished at us. She remained in the same condition Friday night and Saturday. There were a great many came to see her, among them the tavern keeper. He had never seen one under the influence of *that* kind of spirit before ; he tried to bend her little finger. I didn't see her after we left Bro. Ward's until Sunday morning. It appeared that she remained in the same state all day Saturday and all night, making four days and five nights.— Sunday morning she revived, happy in God, and perfectly well. She felt no inconvenience from lying so long on the floor, or going without food. She remembered that the coffee hurt her, and also the moving. When Adams tried to bend her finger it hurt her, and her finger was lame and sore for some time. All that were present Sunday saw that the " dead was alive again," for such exhortation, I hardly ever heard before. She upbraided the people for their unbelief in her case as well as in others of a similar character, where God had ' slain' the body, to subdue pride. She was conscious nearly or quite all the time, and knew what was going on, and why she couldn't move. She had been opposed

to " losing her strength," and fought against it.
But when she came to the conclusion that she
would not fight God's Spirit any longer, let it
do what it would, she *fell* under it. But pride
still worked, and she was, some of the time,
ashamed of her position, and was unwilling to
yield. Then she would be stiffened and feel
worse, and then when she consented to have the
Spirit work *any* way, she felt better. She said
that God kept her in that situation until she
was fully subdued, and was willing to be a fool
for Christ's sake. These are her words. She
has lived her religion ever since, or till the last
time I saw her, which was some six years after
this. She had married a Methodist minister,
and was a great help to him in the work of God,
and I have heard of them since as being yet at
work. Come skeptic, what say you to this, guilty or not guilty? You will plead not guilty of
course. But the day is near when God will
show you that your reasoning from a cold and
wicked heart will not answer your purpose. I,
and hundreds of others know these things to be
true, and are willing to meet them in the judgment. In those days it was no uncommon thing
to see demonstrations of the power of God upon
the human system among all denominations that
were not dead or frozen together with formality. Some may say, these things happened, before people were enlightened, and as fast as
people get educated these things disappear.—

So they do, and the vitality of godliness with them. For the wise of the world always overlook the simplicity of the gospel, and therefore becomes blind to things of God, and call them foolishness, when in fact, they were the fools. This class of wise fools existed in Christ's day, and for the want of godly knowledge, they crucified the Lord of glory. Read the second chapter of first Corinthians, and you will see who knew the most about the knowledge of God's ways, a few ignorant fishermen, or the D. D.s of that age. If this is sound reasoning to say, the more education, the more religion, then you should look to this wise republic, to find a holy place, and what *do* you find ? one of the most wicked places under heaven, except a convent, or combination of Catholic priests. Look at the city of Washington, and the Senate and House of Representatives. Every commandment of God is broken by that body.

But to proceed with camp-meeting interest. In the year of '43, in May, I took a lease of a Mr. Potter, of Palmer, of a piece of land, for a camp-meeting. It began in spirit, and went on in power. Many who were there, will recollect that this was the time that Bro. K. S. Hastings prayed nearly an hour, and God shook the whole encampment, and many fell prostrate in front of the stand, which were the best notes that this man of God could have before him while preaching. Father Wm. Miller was at the meeting, but did not oppose the work, although he never saw it in that fashion before. One young woman rose up, while under an exercise, and pointed her finger at a wicked rowdy, and he fell as quick as if a bullet had hit him. He came forward for prayers, and many others. He was converted, and told me that nothing ever set his sins in such a light before him, as that did. He was satisfied that the hand of God was in it. He was a perfect stranger to this young woman. She lived in Middletown, and was very deaf. She had heard nothing that he had said that caused this involuntary movement of the hand, and she was tried about it afterwards. This was the meeting where one of the backslidden sisters was found in the woods by some men who supposed she was dying. Her groans attracted them to the spot. She didn't speak, or pay any attention to them, and they came to the camp-ground and told me that there was a woman down in the woods, dying. Myself and another man went down to see, and as soon as we got within hearing, the thing was revealed to us, and when we arrived there, prayer was offered, without any conversation with her, and God set the dying woman at liberty again. This was a strange thing to the men. Why didn't they know what ailed her? They had *worldly* wisdom enough, for they appeared to have come from the "Minister Factory," in Wilbraham, a few miles off. Why

not know what the work of God was? I will
let Paul answer. See 1 Cor. ii : 11.

I shall be obliged to omit many things. I
have written much already that skeptics will not
believe ; but this book is not designed to please
any one in particular, and as I shall lose nothing,
and do not expect to gain anything, I will relate another circumstance which took place at
this meeting. Among the wheat or good things,
there are tares or wicked things. The " Cain
family" acted like their father Cain : They got
mad because " Abel's family" got the blessing.
One of them was uglier than the rest, and had
been all through the meeting. He picked up a
pocket-book containing money and some valuable papers in it, and refused to give it up. I
was informed of the fact, and set to work to get
it. I asked counsel of a lawyer on the ground
by the name of Rogers. He didn't think it
worth while to do anything, for the fellow had
a right to keep it for a certain length of time.
But this didn't satisfy me. I believed that I
could get it. Knowing that he was a rowdy,
I expected that he would do something that
would justify me in putting him into the preachers' stand, which was our prison at camp-meetings. I kept watch of him, and soon saw him
throw a stick in a tent where there was a pray-
er-meeting. This was enough. I laid hands
on him, and took him to the stand : he was
down at the mouth immediately, and wanted to

know what he had done. I told him that he had *stolen* a pocket-book, and thrown sticks into a tent, &c., and that he was now detected, and would be dealt with accordingly. He said that he *found* the pocket-book, and told where, which I knew was true. He told the truth, and was willing to give the pocket-book to me. I then called in Mr. Rogers the lawyer, to hear the statement, and he said that I had fairly outwitted the fellow, and was safe in taking the pocket-book, as I had the charge of the meeting and a lease of the ground. I took it, counted the money, and gave it to the owner the next day. The lawyer talked with him, and he promised to behave, if I would let him go, which I did for that time. The next night, about two o'clock, the whole encampment was awakened by some one near by cursing and swearing, and making all kinds of noises. He soon came on to the ground, and the watch couldn't still him. They threatened to call me. He damned me and every body else, and defied any one to lay hands on him, &c. I lay and heard it for some time. Bro. Hawks spoke to me, and said that there was a job for me, and I began to think so, for I was out of patience just at that time. I got up, and in my hurry put on one of Bro. Hawks' boots, and went out of the tent just as he said he wanted to see the committee. I made myself acquainted with him very suddenly. Being out of patience, I made him take some

L. OF C.

very long and singular steps off the ground.—
I wanted no help, and told the brethren to go
back on their watch. I took him off down the
road, over the hill, some 15 or 20 rods : he
tried to yet away, but had stopped swearing,
and had no desire to see the committee. I discovered a sprout that had been broken off from
a walnut stump, and I took it up. I thought
it just the thing for him, and let him have it
around the legs. He struck at me, but his arm
was too short to hit me. I put the sprout on
until he begged. It was daybreak then, and as
he promised good behavior, I was about to let
him go, but just then I discovered that he was
the very one that I let off the day before that
had taken the pocket-book. He had broken his
promise once, and I thought he might again,
and as the sprout held good, I gave him another
lacing, until he appealed to my *Christianity* for
mercy, saying, " If you are a Christian, *do* stop,"
when I let him go, upon his promising again to
go off and be peaceable, which he did : he went
as far as I could see him, and didn't look back.
When I came in sight of the ground, there were
half a dozen or more of my brethren, who had
been looking over the hill all the time. Hence
it was not as private as I expected. Some of
them say to this day, that I said when I came
back that I flogged him in the name of the
Lord ; but I do not remember it. John Ord-
way said that I certalnly did say so, and others

heard it ; so I shall not deny it. These are the facts in this case, that so many have heard of, and may have asked me about it : now it is made public. This worked a lasting reformation *on* him, if not *in* him, for he has always behaved well ever since. He never has denied being the one that Munger whipped. I should not know him now ; but probably he yet remembers me, although it is more than eleven years ago. There is something singular in my case that astonishes others as well as myself.— When I look back, and see the continual hatred manifested towards me by the " Cain family," and the various plots and plans that have been laid by them, at different times, to revenge themselves upon me, it seems as if God had helped me ; for I never have had a drop of my blood spilled, nor have I been hurt in any way whatever by them, although it has been reported that I have been whipped a number of times, and there was great rejoicing with the enemies of God, and such have always been my enemies. I never have begun anything of the kind without accomplishing it sooner or later.

At a camp-meeting in Westfield, a rowdy struck me while he was passing in a wagon, and then drove off at full speed. I told the people that I should find him out sooner or later.— About fourteen years after, a man came and acknowledged the deed. A man named Murphy heard him relate this story, and as he thought that I was dead or had gone off, he felt quite safe until Murphy told him that I lived within two miles of him, and that he was not safe unless he settled it with me. He told him many awful things about me that were *not true,* on purpose to see what effect it would have upon the fellow. It scared him so, that he came up to see me, but I was not at home. He came the second time, and wanted it settled. I had given this case up, years before, and it came very unexpected to me. It *was* settled before he went off, and that was the last that I ever heard of him. Another time, I was helping survey some land on the rail-road, and the surveyer called me by name. I told him that I didn't remember him. He said, he did me, and said that a number of years before that, I took him at a camp-meeting as a prisoner, handled him very roughly, and put him into the preachers' stand. But he succeeded in getting out in my absence, and ran away out of the place to get rid of the scrape. He soon saw the folly of his course, and turned over a new leaf. He was very good natured about it, and found no fault with me. His name was Phelps. He was worth considerable property, and had a large salary yearly. I could multiply such cases, some on steam-boats, rail-roads and various other places in other states. I have met with similar receptions from people that I had long before forgotten. All this leads me to wonder that I have

not been killed, when I see so many straight
and dangerous places that I have been through,
with the hatred of the "Cain family." Three
times, a dirk has been drawn on me, and once a
jack-knife. But, thank God, I continue to this
day, safe and sound, and am at war with the
devil, his works, and his workmen, and always
shall be, I hope, while I live here in this state
of temptations and trials. I have one consola-
tion, the "Cain family" do not like me, and I do
not feel like compromising with them, at the expense of truth, righteousness and morality. I
will close the "stick and whipping" part of this
narrative, by saying to all that I have dressed
down in various ways in this and other places,
It has been for *your good*. I consider it a better, shorter, and cheaper way than to commence
a suit against you, and so I have no account un-
settled up to date.

I will now proceed yet farther with camp-
meetings : for a few months I cannot recollect
dates, for it was about the time that I attended
ten in one year. I attended one at Walling-
ford, Ct., and I think it was the same year of
the last mentioned. This was characterized by
a number of strange things. It was about the
time that the Lord was expected, in '44. All
the Advent presses stopped, and it was *generally* believed that our warfare was nearly at a
close, and of course there would be much excitement and honesty, and so it was. It was

at this meeting that one of the rowdies had been threatening what he would do, and said that *he* WOULD do so and so, if he went to *hell*. But he failed of doing what he proposed, for he fell from a high mill-dam the day that the meeting begun and broke his neck, and died on the spot. This secured us good order during the meeting. The work of getting ready to meet the Lord was of the utmost importance, and all felt it. I never saw so solemn a place before ; scores confessing their faults, and asking each other's forgiveness ; sinners forward for prayers in every tent, and men trying to give their money away to any one who would take it. I saw a large pile of bank bills on the preachers' stand that no one would take. Calls were made a number of times, for any one that wished, to come and take what they had a mind to. It seemed that no one dare take a dollar of it unless they needed it for immediate use. Such was the honesty, that it carried conviction to the hardest sinners' hearts, and many wept to see the sight. None dare take the money not even the wicked. It was a godly sacrifice, offered in good faith and honesty. Soon after breakfast one morning, a young woman of excellent character and unassuming appearance, had an exercise that astonished all present. About ten rods from the encampment she "lost her strength," and began talking in an unknown tongue. No one present understood it, but there was a power in

it, that made all feel that the Lord ordered it
for good. Sinners quailed under it, and all won-
dered what this strange thing meant, especially
those who were acquainted with the modesty of
the one speaking, for she was very bashful. Her
face looked like an angel of light, while speaking. I knew her at *Middletown*, and was astonished when I was told who it was, for her
appearance was very much changed. She talked
a number of different languages, so said good
judges, for she had everybody on the ground
to hear her—good and bad, learned and ignorant. This phenomena continued four hours
and forty minutes. All this time she stood out
in the sun bare headed, and talked very fast.
When she had done speaking, she seemed to be
perfectly well, and unexhausted. What this
thing meant, *I* never knew, and no one else
pretended to account for it. A number dated
their convictions from this scene. This young
woman did not know what she said, but knew
what she meant, for her message was to the people there, and she couldn't help talking, and
made no effort of her own to commence or stop.

Soon after this, there was baptizing nearly
all day, for every person wanted to do their
duty. There was a sermon preached on baptism, showing that immersson was the only
scriptural mode, and nearly a hundred went
into the water, old and young, and most of them
came out shouting. The meeting continued

interesting to its close and much good was done, although some fanaticism was discovered, as is usual on such occasions of excitement. Many will recollect this meeting as being the most exciting one of this age. Many things I have probably forgotten, which others will remember, when they read this account. Brn. Hawks, Allen, and G. Miller went to this meeting from this place, and perhaps others who will know all these facts, as well as I do.

The next meeting that I shall give an account of, was the second meeting held at Chester factories. There was little of much importance here, but one thing I will mention.— The "Cain family" determined to break up our meeting, the last night, and it appeared that there were *two* to our *one*. I felt that God would help us out of trouble if I would go into the tent and pray. This was an uncommon impression for me to have, and I tried to get rid of it, but couldn't. I told sister Wait how I felt, and she told me to go, and she would take the light, stand out among the rabble, and take my place. I went into the tent, and remember of seeing Bro. Mathewson there, when I got down to pray, and how long I prayed or what for, except for God to chain the wicked, I do not know. Sister Wait said that there wasn't a thing done while I was praying. There seemed to be a chaining influence among them. This was a strange exercise of mind for me, but

it was all that I had to do about keeping order
that night. I think that Bro. Mathewson
preached; at any rate, others took hold, after
I had done praying, and God gave us the victory. The "Cainites" all went off in such a
hurry that they forgot to take their implements
of war, part of which were about a peck of eggs.
The next morning we found them, and as they
were all good, they were all put to a good use,
that is, cooked, to feed the saints their last meal
on that ground. Truly, the wicked fled, that
time, when no man pursued.

I continued going to meetings most of the
time for a long while. I recollect of coming
home about those times from a long tour all
worn down. I had been to Middletown with
Bro. K. S. Hastings. I took my wife, and
started to visit her friends, and rest awhile. On
our way we heard of a protracted meeting on
that road, and thought we would stop a short
time. Sister Higgins was lecturing. After
the lectures, liberty was given to pray and exhort as the Spirit moved. Some prayed; but
it seemed to be a dead set. When the man of
the house, being a preacher, requested me to
take hold, I told him that I was worn out, and
was going further that night, and must be off.
But he was very urgent, and I told him that
the meeting was prayed to death, and that such
prayers as were then being offered would kill
any meeting. The sister prayed for everything

that she could think of, and then repeated them over again. I told Bro. P. that I would stop a little while, and make a few remarks on long praying, &c. I got tired of waiting for her to finish, and cried out, " Lord, bless that sister *now,* so that she can stop praying ?" She stopped, and I talked short and plain. I told them what killed the meeting, and then we started a class-meeting. I spoke to some whom I knew did not enjoy religion, and was pointed in my remarks : I felt that something might be done. The Spirit of God began to move, and the wicked and triflers began to scatter, and, in a short time, we had a good meeting. As I was going, for I had stayed much longer than I had expected, we got into the entry, and we saw a young woman making sport of some of the expressions I made use of in the meeting. I felt like speaking to her, but it was late, and we had two miles further to go, so we started ; but I wanted to speak to her, and I knew it would take but a moment, so I left my wife standing at the door, and that was the last I saw of her till the next day, for here began a work that took nearly all night to finish. I spoke to the woman, and will give the language as nearly as possible between us. " Young woman, do you enjoy religion ?" " No, sir."— " Did you ever ?" " No, sir." " Do you ever expect to ?" " No, sir." " Do you believe in the Christian religion ?" " Yes, sir." " Do

you believe you will go to hell without it ?"—
"Yes, sir." She was so prompt, that I hardly
knew what question to put next ; but I could
not give it up. I saw that all were still ; they
knew what I had to contend with, but I did
not. Next question : "Do you expect to sin
against such light, and then go to hell after all?"
Answer was very prompt—"Yes, sir." "Do
you believe that God will answer the prayers of
his people ?" "Yes, sir, I do." "Well, inas-
much as you *expect* to go to hell, would it not
be appropriate to pray to God to take you away
this night, rather than let you go on in sin any
longer, as your torment would be worse ?"—
"Yes, sir," was the horrid and unexpected reply. I paused, and trembled. "Will you go
and kneel down for me to pray ?" "Yes, sir."
And she did : this was a trying time to all present, saint and sinner. I commenced praying
and telling the Lord what he had heard said by
us both, and prayed that, if it were *possible* to
save this sinner, he would do it now. But, if
not, to answer prayer. At this moment, she
cried out for mercy. Others knelt down, and
God took the work into His hands, and she soon
came out happy, and praised the Lord. She
went to work for others, and God blessed a
number of them. After we closed, I requested
something to eat, and this woman took me into the buttery. She stopped in the kitchen and
embraced her father and mother, rejoicing in

what God had done for her since the meeting
closed. This was the first time that I learnt
that she was Elder P. Powell's daughter. It
always astonishes me when I think of this scene.
I have talked this over with Azuba since, and
she says that God plucked her as a brand from
the fire, for her breath had stopped, and she
would have *died*, if she had not cried out before I had spoken the next word. This was the
work of God, and it was marvelous in *our* eyes.
I saw her father and sister recently, and they
told me that Azuba was trying to live religion.
This circumstance took place about ten years
ago, at Three Rivers, in Palmer, Mass.

About this time, I heard from my brother who
had been gone twelve years. He had wander-
ed around like the prodigal son, and he had done
worse than to *feed* swine, for he had made himself one by intemperance. I found him at Niagara a confirmed infidel ; he worked Sundays,
swore about Christianity, and forbade his family
attending meeting. But his wife and eldest
daughter had disobeyed him when he was gone,
and had made a profession of religion, which enraged him so, that he forbade their attending
church or praying in his house. This was the
state that I found him in. After talking over
old times, his wife opened her book of sorrows
to me, and said that her conviction was so great
that she had concluded to commit suicide, and
once opened the door to throw her girl into the

river, and then jump in herself. She showed me the place. The house stood on the bank of the east branch of the Niagara river, and a few rods above the falls, and near the grist mill, so it would have been sure death to both of them. She told me that she opened her door and took hold of her girl, but the child mistrusted that all was not right, and took hold of the rocking-chair to prevent her mother throwing her in. She tried in vain to unclinch her hands, and the child screaming, " Don't drown me, mother !" so affected her, that she shut the door, surprised that the child should mistrust her design.— After hearing this sad tale, I had all that I could bear. Lucia had been telling me her troubles which showed out *some* of his tyranny, but kept others back on my account. I had not yet introduced the subject of religion, for she told me that I could not pray in the house, if he was present. I told her that I could stay but two days, and I should not leave without praying, and that he was not able to put me out, and I *should* pray that night, if God so directed, and if I called on her to pray, she must follow. She dared not promise. She believed God had sent me there for *some* purpose. He came in from work, (this was Sunday evening,) for he worked all day in the mill. After supper, I inquired if there was a meeting in the place. On learning that the Methodists had one, I requested them all to go. This was a curious request

to my brother ; but as I had come over four
hundred miles to see him, he consented to go.
We arrived at the house, and he seated me.—
The people looked astonished to see *that infidel*
in meeting. after saying and doing what *he* had.
However, the meeting commenced. I soon saw
that it was a general class-meeting. The leader
seemed to dread to come to us, not knowing
who I was, but supposed I was a friend of that
infidel, Munger ; and *if* so, we were no friends
to God or his cause. But he ventured up, and
spoke to my brother first, as he was on the end
of the seat. He told the class-leader that he
had not altered his mind, and did not want any
conversation, for he only came in with his brother (pointing to me,) and said that *I* would
turn in a hand, or something similar. I arose
and had uncommon liberty. I saw that the
effect was good on the congregation : it allayed
their fears in regard to us, if nothing more.—
His wife and daughter cried for joy or fear, which
made him uneasy ; but he staid until meeting
was out. After we got home, we talked awhile
about home and friends. I called for his Bible,
read and prayed without consent or molestation.
I then called upon his wife, and she ventured
to begin for the first time before her wicked
husband, and had disobeyed his commands. I
felt confident that he would not disturb us :
and after his wife had finished praying, I called
on his daughter with the same confidence that

she would pray unmolested, which she did very feelingly. She prayed for her father, which caused him to hitch in his chair, and I saw that he had got " a hook in his jaw :" I thanked God, and took courage. I slept with him that night, for the sake of talking about home, &c., but did not feel at liberty to introduce the subject of religion at all. The next day, we went over into Canada, saw the great falls and other curiosities ; but all the time felt no liberty to say anything about religion. We went home, and at the table he wished me to ask a blessing.— This affected his wife, as she never expected to see any alteration in him ; and this was the reason why she determined to commit the rash act of drowning herself and child, rather than live as she had done. I told her that God had begun to work with him, and he would have to come down. We all prayed that night. This was the last night that I was going to stay with them, and it was affecting even to him ; but he suppressed his feelings. I slept with him that night, but did not mention the subject of religion to him *then*. He was uneasy in the night, rested but little, and in the morning was very different. He consented to go sixty miles with me to a place called Holland's Purchase, now called Batavia, to look up some relatives. On the way, we had occasion to travel on foot about four miles. I felt it duty *then* to talk upon the subject of religion, and he lent a listening ear,

and, for the first time in his life, had a disposition to read the Bible. We spent an hour and
a half under a large tree, and God began to
work visibly. I had liberty in talking then, and
he acknowledged that he wanted religion, but
would not consent to pray; but I persuaded
him not to prevent his wife and daughter praying. I told him that his wife consented to set
up the altar till he forbade it. She said that
she would pray that night; and I made him
promise that he would encourage his wife and
daughter. I gave him my Bible, and bade him
farewell, and told him that unless he repented,
God would trouble him. As I stepped into the
cars, I saw the tears start as he turned to go away.
I felt very sure that he had a load to carry home
such as he never had before. The letters which
I had from them soon after told the story; I
wish I had them recorded verbatim in this work,
but they are lost. But it was as follows :—
After he arrived at home, his wife saw such a
difference in him, that she was not afraid to fulfill her promise to me that she would pray that
night, which she did, and God took him in hand
in good earnest. His convictions were so great
that it seemed to him that he must die before
morning. The neighbors came in, and all the
different preachers prayed with him, and I think
it was not till the next day that he found relief.
God showed him to his content and heart-felt
sorrow what it was to be an infidel. He little

thought that God was going to work in that way
when he consented to let his wife and daughter
pray. But his letter to me was full of thankfulness and praises to God that I ever hunted
him up, and took the course that I did ; for, if
I had crowded the subject too fast, he should
have resisted ; but, strange as it may seem to
some, was blessed of God. He often spoke of
the little red-covered Bible that I gave him,
and the promise which he made to me in return,
and thanked God in his last letter for the two
days' interview that I had with him. He went
still farther west, and from there started for Cali-
fornia, and I have reasons to believe that he died
on the road, as nothing has been heard from him
for a number of years. But I feel that I did
my duty ; for God converted him, and it was
his duty to *keep* converted by obedience, which
he did the last I heard of him, and I hope to
meet him in the kingdom of God when it is set
up.

The next season after I visited Niagara, I
hired a piece of ground for a camp-meeting in
Manchester, Ct., in '43. The meeting progressed in spirituality, and the " Cainites," as
usual, commenced " swearing their prayers,"
and making disturbance. I thought that the
shortest way would be, to run the ring-leader
down the hill. I got behind him, and started
him so suddenly that his companions could not
help him. He resisted what he could, but could

' not turn round, for I was behind him, and had hold of both arms, and on a good speed down the hill. He cried out for help, and the rabble came, like so many demons. I gave him a push, and he went headlong over the fence at the bottom of the hill. I dodged behind a tree when I pushed him, and his companions supposing ◆ that it was *me* who was down, jumped on him and beat him unmercifully, so that he got more pay in his OWN coin than he bargained for. He went home not thinking much of the blessings of camp-meetings. In a day or two, the rabble assembled again, and just as they got near the ground, God sent one of the heaviest thunder storms that I ever saw. They ran in every direction—some for home, others for the tavern which was about a half mile off; some came on the ground, and I took pains to invite them into the tents that did not leak, and then, set the prayer meetings going in *those* tents in particular. Many of these fellows appeared serious, and as they were used well, concluded to go home peaceably, which they did. This ended the rowdyism of this meeting. But there was some *skepticism* left, which God only could cure. There was one of those dandy professors squinting about, to find something to find fault with. If any one was "slain," or shouted, he would question the propriety of such things. He was told, that *his* religion lay in the propriety of finding fault with others. He was exhorted and advised to seek God, and get religion, for it was evident that he did not know what it was. He kept around in the way, all day, and saw Brn. Allen and Anderson *jump* when they exhorted. This was also as strange as losing their strength. He finally said, that if these things were a reality, he wished that he might have it, and appeared serious about it. Soon after, a prayer meeting commenced at the stand, and when it got well agoing, I heard some one cry out for the Lord to help, and save them. I knew that God had taken *some* one in hand by the way they cried. On going to the stand, there, to my surprise, lay that dandy professor, wallowing in the dirt and taking on bitterly.— His clean nankeen pants, and gentlemanly, fault-finding religion, fared something alike ; neither were worth but little after God took him in hand. Many will recollect this circumstance. I believe that there are thousands of professors, who never saw themselves sinners, and know nothing of conversion.

In those days, I went to meeting so much that I got worn out, and my financial affairs needed my attention, for this was the time that people who were dishonest could take advantage of the *rogues' law*, known as the "assignment law." I had nearly all that I was worth out in debts. One after another that owed me, signed over, and I lost in every way. Some that owed me were honest, but could not pay. I held notes of $400 against one person, but gave them up, without receiving a cent. Another owed me $65. Then down went D. and J. Ames, which was worse than *all* the rest, and so on until I lost all that I was worth, which was about $1.500. I had, at this time, a large family of little children, and had to move out of the house that I had labored hard to build, for a shelter for my family. I hired a tenement in the village. But soon sickness set in, and death entered the family circle, and in less than eighteen months, it robbed us of three children, two in one week : this was in '46. This was a time of trouble, and the Lord only knew what we should do, for I did not. Property all gone, and death doing its work. I was in debt, and but very few *true* friends, for I could not even get the use of a meeting house to have the funeral services in ; I tried the Methodist and Baptist, but was denied. I thought of Job, and read it. But God raised up one friend that helped me in this time of affliction. That was Harvey Holkins of Warehouse Point. He at different times, let me have $150 without any security, and ran the risk, (for it was a risk) of getting his pay. He has not got it yet, nor even *mentioned* it to me ; but I have mentioned it to *him*. Many poor people that have been in trouble, can thank God for his having a charitable heart. His faith was shown by his works, and is *yet*. May the Lord reward him. In those two years I invented a water-wheel, got it patented in the fall of '46, and in '47 we moved to New Hampshire. I took some mills in company with Timothy Cole, and put in a number of my patent wheels, and procured a good living, without getting in debt. But we were all homesick, for part of our family were buried in Massachusetts, and their graves often came to our remembrance, and I made arrangements to sell out and come back, which I did in a short time, and had something left for my creditors. I always said that I never would take the benefit of the bankrupt law, and I kept my word, although I was advised to do it, and out of $600 that I received for my profit on the patent. I gave up $400 to be distributed among my creditors as they saw fit. Some still hold small demands against me. but I feel justified with the course that I took in regard to money matters, and can look any man in the face, for I have done all that I could, thus far, and still mean to, for I am not trying to lay up a treasure *here.*

On returning from New Hampshire, sickness again entered the family. The first week it was the varioloid, and one girl seven years old, had the small-pox, and died. I was in N. H. on business, and never saw her after I left home.— This makes five children out of eight, that have died, leaving only three. So all can see that I have had my share of trouble, and do fully realize that the curse is not yet removed, and I

long for the time to come, when death, and him
that hath the power over it. which is the Devil,
shall be destroyed. This time is soon coming,
and all Bible Christians know that their reward comes then, and not before, Catholics and
spiritualists to the contrary notwithstanding.
God's word will stand.

While in New Hampshire I attended meeting
somewhere nearly every Sabbath, but religion
was at a very low ebb in that region ; my being
a stranger, and my coarse uncouth way, pre-
vented me in a great measure from being as ac-
tive as where I was known. But I will state
two circumstances which took place while I
lived there. The first was in Lake village.—
While on business there, I learnt that there
was dissatisfaction in the place about two soci-
ties coming together. ·The facts were these :
The regular Baptists had got so low that they
could not support a minister, and made a pro-
position to the Free-will Baptists to meet with
them if they would, and take the choir off their
hands that was already hired for a year. This
included one or two fiddlers as wicked as Cain,
as is generally the case. To this, some of the
old fathers of the Free-will Baptist church objected, and argument was used on both sides.
I offered to deliver a lecture on instrumental
music in the church on Sabbath evening. The
arrangements were made, and the notice given
out, and there was a general turn out. I went

on to show by the Scripture, that instrumental music was first invented and used by the Cain family—the sons of old Jubal, see Gen. 4: 21, and ought always to be kept there. I showed that David backslid in consequence of his fiddling disposition, and showed how, and where ; and also Solomon after he backslid, went into instrumental music, and that of all sorts. See Eccl. 2: 8, and the fiddling spirit was what caused the low state of religion in the Baptist church in that place, and it always did in old times. I then quoted Amos 5: 23, to show that God would not smell in the assemblies where their songs were identified with the sound of fiddles, or viols, and it is *now*, as it was *then*—it is offensive to the nostrils of the Almighty, and then quoted Amos, 6th chapter, 1–6, to exhibit the condition of the church in olden times, for following the examples of David. God pronounced a curse upon them, and he has not changed any since, and even where fiddling was tolerated there would be a backslidden state of the church, or at ease in Zion. The teachings of Christ and the Apostles did not mention it, which they would have done if it belonged to divine worship. But they knew that it belonged to the other side of the house. All that were godly, and had consulted the Scriptures, could now see that the curses of God follow the Cain family's practice, &c. I then took up the character of some of the fiddlers in *our* State. They would raise the devil all the week, get drunk Saturday night, swear their prayers, calling on God to damn their souls, &c., and Sunday morning, get up just in time to go to the house of God, and take the lead of the religious services. Just at that time a man arose and said it was *"a damned lie,"* and then left the house, swearing and scolding. I waited a moment and then proceeded, having a good chance to make the application, which I improved, and gave way for remarks from others, which resulted in the dismissal of the fiddlers from the Free will Baptist church. This man that went out swearing, was the very character that I had described, and was the first fiddler. He took the lead of singing. He was drunk the night before, which was Saturday night, and had been fiddling that day in the place, with the expectation of a year's job, and then to have his plans upset, it was more than he could bear patiently. " I'll lick that man," said he. " But you can't do it," said another. " Then d—n him, I'll kick him, and run." I knew nothing about the character of *their* fiddlers until after the meeting was out, and then members of the Free will Baptist church told me the above facts. The next day I came away, and have not seen the place since. I had a letter from there soon after, stating that the fiddlers in Zion were down on me, for they had lost their job.

I will mention one more circumstance that took place while I lived in N. H., which may not be amiss. Just before leaving the State, I had occasion to go to the upper part of it on business. On learning that a Dr. Kelly, who had moved from our State and town, lived up still further, I went to see him. The family knew me while fifty rods or more from the house, although it was a number of years since we had met. My dress has always been of the same fashion, which will account for this in part. The doctor was gone, and I was uneasy, but could not get back that night, for the cars had gone the last time for that day ; so I made myself as contented as I could, and in our conversation it was mentioned that there was a camp-meeting being held about two miles still further north, and to pass the time off, I went up. I have forgotten the name of the place, but it was on the right hand track, from fifty to seventy miles from Concord. I arrived at the ground about 5 o'clock, P. M. It was rainy, and there was preaching in two or three tents. I listened to a sermon on holiness which had much more of the letter in it than the spirit. After preaching, I looked around the ground, but could see no one that I knew, or ever saw before. This was something new to have all strangers to me on a camp-ground. I was homesick, and started to go back to Dr. Kelly's ; but seeing a good fire, I stopped to warm me, and engaged in conversation with a good Christian, no doubt, but rather a simple one. He said to me, "It is rather rainy." I answered, "Yes." He then asked me where I came from. I told him. He then wanted to know if I enjoyed religion. I evaded the question in part, seeing what he was. He then told *his* experience, and questioned me closely. I gave him to understand that I professed religion, but did not have much enjoyment there, for I was among strangers, &c. This made him the more interested in my case. He said there was going to be a general class-meeting in the preachers' tent, and showed it to me. I learned that it was a class of young preachers that came from Concord. He was so anxious about me, that I told him I would go into the class-meeting a little while, as he thought I might get blessed. When the singing commenced we went in. There were three rows of seats, and I took one in the middle row, near the door. After prayer by one of the young preachers, the meeting commenced : I soon saw that it was no place for me. The preacher was a dandy-looking fellow ; had a fine cane which he hooked onto his arm, while leading the class.

Ten or fifteen spoke ; but not one spoke of having any enjoyment. If they *had*, I should not have believed them, for their silks, bows and ribbons spoke as clearly as they did, of no religious enjoyment. In reply to any of them, the leader would say, " Go on, brother," or " sister."

That was to encourage them in their backslidden state which they acknowledged they were then in. I thought " Good Lord, where is Methodism !" and was about starting to leave, when to my astonishment, the leader touched me on the shoulder, and desired me to lead the rest of the class. He thought by my dress that I was a Methodist; I suppose.

I had to think quick ; but I arose, and in short told my experience with Methodism, and soon felt the burden of the meeting upon me. I spoke to one, and she said that she did not enjoy anything. I told her that I knew it before she arose. I spoke to the second : she hesitated, but finally arose, and said that she must say what the first one did. I reproved her sharply, and called upon the third. This was a dead set ; she would not stir. I felt like talking, and told them that I had not heard one speak of any religious enjoyment, and they were a pack of proud backsliders. God gave me great plainness of speech, and liberty while talking. I looked at the fellow who was so anxious about my welfare, and you can judge how astonished he looked. I then proposed clearing one of the middle seats, and called all forward who said they wanted prayers ; for when they spoke, they all closed by saying, " I desire your prayers that I may be more faithful," &c. This expression was a *habit*, not sincere, and unless they took that seat, it was proved that they didn't mean what

they said, and honesty was the first step towards
getting blessed : and I told the whole tent's
company that God would work, if they would
let him. I commenced singing, and they began
coming forward. This young dandy preacher
looked very strange ; but I had got the meeting in hand, and he saw it. Soon the seat was
nearly filled, and I told them that God would
bless all that were willing to ask him, and that
all could pray at once, for it was no confusion
to the Lord. We knelt down before God, and
I led in prayer. Soon the work of God broke
out, and a number were praying at the same
time. The work increased, and others came
forward : there was a general cry all over the
tent. Some were slain. I scarcely ever saw
the power of God more manifest than on that
occasion. The one that I spoke to, who would
not come forward nor arise, was slain where she
was. This was an old-fashioned Methodist meeting. It did me good to see the gauzes, ribbons,
and starched dresses lay in the wet straw. Many came out happy and shouting, and went to
praying for others. I thought I would leave
the tent, which I did, very suddenly, and no
one noticed it, as I sat near the end. I started
for Dr. Kelly's in the dark, and I never felt more
sensibly the blessing of God, than I did all the
way to the Dr's I could hear them shout when
a mile off. I was wet through, and the doctor
wanted to give me some medicine, for fear that

I should take cold. But I told him that God had so blessed me I should not take cold. I went to bed but could not sleep for rejoicing.— I started home in the first morning train of cars. The whole encampment was searched over to find that stranger that led the class. He was described as a tall man, wore a broad-brimmed hat, &c. No one knew him nor where he came from, except the weak man, that I have mentioned, and *he* did not know when I went out, nor where I had gone. A great deal of anxiety was felt to know who that was that started the meeting where God blessed so many. But I was 100 miles from there by 2 o'clock, and never saw but one man who was at that meeting, and that was about a week after. This man saw me in the city of Manchester, N. H., and knew me by my hat. He ventured into conversation, and asked me if I attended such a camp-meeting.— I told him that I did, and then the mystery was revealed to him. He told me what took place after I left. The work did not stop, although they were all very anxious to know where that strange man was. The work continued that day, which was the last day of the meeting.— God got all the glory *that* time, for no one knew *who* or *where* the instrument was. I do not suppose that such narratives will suit every body, and don't care, for I am independent, and state facts that have taken place in my experience. Some will read this who have seen just

such things in times of revivals, when God had
a fair chance at the hearts of men, and was not
kept back from doing his work in his own way,
as is the case now-a-days. There is so much
fancy kind of religion, and popular chit-chat
that will not hurt the feelings, or disturb the
sinner, that it is sickening to any Christian of
the old stamp.

After I came back from New Hampshire, in
1849, my temporal business was about the same;
just as much as I could do to get a living, and
travel as much as I did to attend meetings
and my business. There has nothing of much
importance occurred at camp-meetings and
other religious meetings of late.

One thing I will mention. About this time,
I took a lease of a piece of land for a camp-
meeting in North Wilbraham. The meeting
commenced, and went on well, and but very
little rowdyism until Friday, when one of the
Cainites made some disturbance at the water,
while the ordinance of Baptism was being ad-
ministered. I did not want to have another
scrape with this class, for I had got tired of always having the burden of the meeting upon
me. But it was no time to back out, *then*.—
This fellow came on the ground, and wanted to
find the committee. He was referred to me.
He wanted to hire that coop, pointing to the
preachers' stand, to put one of his company in
who was drunk, until he got over it. I told

him, *that* was the place where we put *rogues*,
and it was not to be let. He swelled up and
said that he should like to see a man or any
number of men that could put *him* into it. I
told him that *I* had eyed him all day, and if he
did not behave, he *would* see the man that could
put him into it, and he would be the first one
to be put in, too. At this, he made much sport
among his friends, and in the evening came on
the ground, with some others, and commenced
throwing sticks at Bro. King S. Hastings who
was in a prayer meeting. But that old soldier
did not break down for that, for he had stood
and faced a shower of stones once before, when
every other preacher had left the stand. I
knew that small sticks would not drive him out,
but these fellows were bent upon seeing if I
dare keep my word. As soon as things were
ready, I took the first man that attempted to
pick up another stick, by the shoulders. He
felt it, and made a fuss, and out came one after
another from the tent. I stood at the door and
passed a number over to the officer, and pointed out others who were taken care of, for we
were all ready before we commenced. Soon this
great brag came out of the tent, (for they had
gone into the meeting and were making sport,)
and wanted to know what the trouble was. I
told him that, *that* coop was ready for him, took
hold of him, and ordered the iron wristbands to
be put upon him. He tried to show his strength

and courage by resisting, but it was of no use ;
he was the first man that was put into the coop,
as I had said that day. In the morning he was
a sober boy. He begged so hard, promised so
fair, and said that he knew me, and his father
and I were good friends, and both belonged to
the Methodist church. He told me his name.
I was surprised to find that Elijah Plumley had
such a son. But he was humbled, and willing
to pay anything to settle it, so I let him off by
paying the cost of the officers. His neighbors
told me that it was the best thing that ever
happened to him, for he behaved much better
always after.

I am now within the circle of a few years,
where the account of camp-meetings will not be
so interesting in this region, for rowdyism has
been very much subdued and the religious meetings less interesting. But my course of life has
not changed, neither has my faith in the Scriptures. I believe that I have attended a camp-
meeting every year, but to record any more
would only be a repetition, and I believe in *short*
prayers, sermons, epistles, and books. I have
traveled much, for the last few years, in different places, and I find that the world is grow-
ing wiser in everything but religious matters,
or the work of godliness. The adulterated state
of religion has made way for nearly everything to
belong to the church, that wishes to, and this lax
state of things I think, is ushered in by reaching

after popularity, which has always loaded the church with a lot of dead lumber, that is worse than nothing. It is a hard matter to find a church that contends for the old landmarks that their fathers ran out. But there are a few left, and I enjoy myself best with such, and seek their company, let me find them where I will.

In this age of improvement, there is an effort to improve religion also. But *this* improvement consists in throwing the cross of Christ out of it, and the resurrection up into the skies, the cardinal doctrines to the four winds, the prophets into the nest of witches and wizards of olden times, and Christ himself among bastards, and his miracles among cheats and satanic wonders. This class, I have been at war with for the last four or five years. They are known by the name of *Rappers*, in this age, but their ancestors had the name of witches and wizards. Since this new array against the Christian doctrine has appeared, I felt it my duty to buckle on what little armor I have, and give them battle, and they will admit, *themselves*, that I have waited for no combined force, but commenced on my own hook, and done all that I could to destroy their fleet, and never have backed out, when *challenged* for a debate.— This, Mr. Morse knows, for he gave me the first challenge. I soon began to lecture upon this subject, and have been into many places, and

done what I could.   To relate here, all that I
have said or published on this subject, would
swell this work beyond the original intention.
In my debates and discussions, I don't pretend
to a display of eloquence or education, for I
have neither, but use only what weapons I have
providentially procured with my limited means.
I will omit all the forms of discussion, and all
that I have published, except one short article,
which was published in the Advent Watchman,
June 28th, 1854.   This will suffice as showing
my mode of defence in a challenge generally.

A SHORT CONTEST WITH THE RAPPERS.

We are commanded to give a reason of our hope or position to every one that asketh us.— A short time since, the Rappers in a certain place procured a lecturer to upset the truth, and establish spiritualism on the ruins thereof. May 20th, in the evening the Rapper spent nearly all his time *squibing* at the few believers he supposed he had before him, and closed by giving notice that the next Saturday evening he would do some great things, tell them some things they never knew, and ask some hard questions, &c.

The time came, and I had an invitation (and a disposition) to be present and see my poor brothers and their doctrine all evaporated into ether. The lecture had commenced when I got there. I will state the sum and substance of the matter as near as I can recollect, to show that God's promise holds good, viz : That he will furnish his children with the necessary reasons or arguments to stand their ground when attacked by the other family, the descendants of Cain. The lecturer strove hard to blend together the *Angelic Communications,* and the *pretended spiritual ones* of this age.

1st question.—Can any one tell me where the first record of an angel can be found? I answered in the Garden of Eden. He denied it by saying it was a cherubim, not an angel, as many supposed.

He then referred to the men that called on Abraham, and took the position, that the communications of all times, came through literal men and they had not changed, and then quoted Ezekiel and others to show what foolish things we were commanded to believe, more ridiculous than we were asked to believe in these days by the spiritualists, and many other things of like import. He then dwelt largely on Corinthians chap. v : 5, to show that a man had an immortal spirit that must be saved in the day of the Lord Jesus, and quoted Stephen and the thief, and Rev. xxii : 9, to show that the spirit of one of the prophets spoke to John, and that the Scriptures were being fulfilled by the pouring out of his spirit in these last days in giving us these spiritual communications that lead to prophesying, dreaming, and miracles. The Witch of Endor was introduced as one of these good mediums that was driven out, or off, for the light she possessed. He wanted to know if the people could not see something in these days that appeared like the work of miracles or to that effect, as it did in the days of Moses in

Egypt. After exhausting his strength of argument and the time, until nearly 10 o'clock at night, he courteously offered the time up to the Advent friend to mend up the great *breach* he had *made* in their foundation, *seemingly.*— One Methodist Bro. arose and took exceptions to his view of the Witch of Endor and the thief on the cross, but thought this was honest, &c. Another undertook to say something, but the time was so far spent that the people were tired out and began to leave the house, and he sat down.

He then called on me at 10. I thought if there was not more than five minutes, I would show myself ready to dissent in sympathy, if nothing more. I told the people it was so late I only had time to say I didn't think the Rappers honest, and wanted it distinctly understood, that I considered them *anti-christ* that was to come in the last days, and deceive if possible, the very elect. That they were a subject of prophecy, and were deceiving and being deceived, and if they would give me a chance, I would track them from the days of Moses in Egypt, down to the present day, as plain as a fox was ever tracked in a new snow, for the Bible which they disregarded, had pointed them out. By this time the people gave attention, and I sat down. He replied, saying, they believed the Bible, and that I had misrepresented them, &c. I then arose and informed the peo-

ple that I was able to prove my statements
from their own papers and admissions in their
great world's convention at Hartford. Ct.; also,
by remarks from the Rappers in other places,
as follows: The Bible is no better authority
for us, than any other old licentious book, not
as good as an almanac; that Christ was a bastard, and that his blood had no more efficacy in
it than the blood of Abel or any other man. I
then repeated, that for any people to make
such remarks as these and others that could be
named, it was imposing upon a religious community to open the Bible to prove anything
they could say, and that they were wolves in
sheeps' clothing. This kindled up a fire that
set the serpents calling for charity, and they
wanted a Christian spirit manifested, and I sat
down. The nest got stirred up by this time
you may depend; one man said he was a citizen of that place, and he had not been imposed
upon by the Rappers taking the Bible, he professed to be a young convert to their views.—
Another said, if this is a Christian spirit, he did
not want it, &c.

I told him that his old brethren that tried to
turn the deputy from the faith, did not fancy
Paul's spirit when he said, "O, full of all subtlety! thou child of the Devil, how long will you
cease to pervert the right ways of the Lord?"
and that old hag of Endor did not fancy the
spirit of Samuel that drove her out of the land.

She was the first female Rapper we read of, and God killed old Saul because he went to consult her about the dead.

I quoted Chronicles x: 13, 14, and argued, as God did not change, he would curse all that consulted the Rappers as he did Saul, for he (Saul) could not tell what form Samuel was of, only as he asked the old witch, nor can any one know which of the spirits are at work except they ask the clairvoiant, an old witch, and they will often lie, and lay it to the spirit then communicating. I then again sat down, thinking perhaps they would think I had said enough ; at least, to let the people know I had no sympathy with them. But they could not let me alone, the speaker wished to inform the people, that some that had been *Adventists* had embraced the views he had held forth that evening, and was among them, addressing his remarks to me.

I felt called upon again to take the floor. I did so, stating, although it was late, I wanted the people to know it was a *fact*, and that I acknowledged it, and that very fact proved my position true, for the Apostle, speaking of these last times, said, " some shall depart from the (belief in the Advent or) *faith*, giving heed to seducing (or rapping) spirits, or doctrines of devils."— These were to be backsliders, and of that class whose consciences would be " seared as with a hot iron, forbidding to marry, and creeping in-

to houses and leading captive silly women," that
they could lead away with divers lusts ; and this
is the exact character of the Rappers in these
days. In connection with that they have got the
same faith that the Shakers and Mormons have,
who believe in talking with the dead and working
miracles. Now read 2 Tim. iii : 1-9, and you
will see the character spoken of in the scriptures,
that stood in the way of the work of God, just
as you Rappers do now. God pity you ! You
are the Anti-christ of the last days, and if you
are honest, it is because God's word is fulfilled
upon you, as he said in 2 Thess. ii : 8-13, and
you are the very people that God has poured
out this strong delusion upon, that you may believe a lie and be damned—because you have
pleasure in unrighteousness and obey not the
truth.

This application made such a stir with the
speaker who gave the challenge to the " Millerites," and wished them to attend, that he forgot his call a few minutes before for a Christian
spirit, and spoke out at the top of his voice, and
said that I was a *liar*. I told him and the rest
that I did not expect they could or would
stand the truth, any more than they would obey
it, and I had used only about fifteen minutes to
answer or reply to what he had said in two hours,
and if they would give me half the time he had
used, I would meet them at any time, and prove
to them who believed in the Bible, that the Rap-

pers were from the same piece as the ancient sorcerers, and are the witches and wizards of the last days, who are to come just previous to the coming of the Lord, and it was one of the strongest signs of the correctness of our position. I then closed, and went to the door, when the sexton came in and told the speaker that he had only hired the hall till nine o'clock, and it was then after ten, and he should put out the lights in a moment or two.

This ended the short battle between truth and error for that time.

If any of the Rappers see this article, just let them recollect that the Advent people are not afraid to meet any or all of them together.

About this time the Maine liquor law question came up. I had always been interested in the subject of temperance after Priest Phenix got me fairly harnessed, as you will recollect.— The Maine law was very unpopular, especially among the rowdies and rummies. I ventured out on that question, and consented to stand as one of the vigilant or prosecuting committee, and endeavored to do my duty. This brought a new class of people to contend with, which made me unpopular with three classes, rappers, rummies and rowdies. I saw that I had got into business, sure enough ; but knowing that I

had made myself ridiculous to this class years
before, I would not back out, and did what I
considered to be my duty, notwithstanding those
influences that were working against me temporally : it made a great difference with me about
obtaining labor and jobs ; but I concluded to
take it easy, and see how the wheel *would* turn.
I would not beg for a job, and some of my near
neighbors who wanted just such work done as
I could do, would give the chance to others instead of me, on account of the strong position
I had taken against the above influences, they
being in sympathy with some or all of the three.
I stood nearly alone for some time, watching human nature. I occasionally went by request to
lecture and hold meetings in different sections,
and took up jobs, if any came in my way. I un-
fortunately got one in the spring of '54, through
the *influence* of a good, honest man ; but I got
into the hands of one of the greatest scoundrels I
have ever met with yet, in all my experience
with mankind. I agreed to get up the machinery for a saw-mill, and start it running, for $1,50
per day, for Nathan Lavee, or *leviathan*, it ought
to be. I went to work immediately, making the
necessary arrangements and contracts, without
any writings, but having good evidence of the bargain ; and it was a short job, only calculated to
last but sixty days. All went on satisfactorily until I was involved in debt $300 for the necessa-
ry machinery for his mill. I called for the mo-

ney to pay for the same, and received $140.—
According to the agreement, he was to pay for
the machinery as fast as I contracted for it,
He at the same time, agreed to get the frame
up for the reception of the machinery when it
was ready. He failed in this, and requested
me to get some one to frame the mill, as he had
failed to get the man that he expected. I got
a man from our place, and took him down there.
All was satisfactory for some time : but soon
the tide turned. The man that Lavee had then
got was the right kind of company ; for Lavee
had told me that he had got a barrel of good
rum, and often asked me to drink. Upon my
refusing, he said that he had got a man that
would drink, as often as he did, and it was
" hail, fellows, well met." The position that I
took against rum drinking did not take with them
at all. We had considerable of conversation
on the subject, and this man that I took down,
knew that I belonged to the vigilant committee
in our place, and had been concerned in spilling
more liquor than they should both want while
they lived. I did not think so much of it then,
for I supposed that Perkins was a friend to me,
for he had worked for me a great deal. I came
home, and sent down the machinery that was
done. I received a letter from Perkins to come
down to the raising. On arriving there, I saw that
the devil had been at work. Every thing, that I
had done was found fault with, and I could do no-

thing right. I learned that in my absence, every
fort had been made to destroy my influence as
a mechanic or Christian. Lavee refused to pay
me anything more, and would not take the machinery I had got for him. I found that he had
told the truth when he said to me previously,
that he supposed God never made another such
an *ugly man* as *he was*, and then told what he
had done. I didn't think much of it then ; but
to my sorrow, I found it to be true. I could
not get him to refer the difficulty to his own
neighbors, nor would he pay one cent. I stayed
over night close by, and took a man with me
to see if *he* could do anything with him in the
morning, for I was in trouble. All the account
not paid would come upon me, and I had nothing to pay with. When we arrived next morning
his wife met us and said that we could do nothing with her husband, for he had been crazy all
night, and had not slept any, or to that effect.
I went in and got my valise : I saw him, and
thought of what he had told me about his being
ugly, for I never saw but one man that showed
the devil in his eyes as he did, and that one was
a *murderer*. I took my valise, and came home,
talked with my creditors, and was advised to sue
him, as it was a clear case ; but I thought of
trying again to settle it, and on the 4th of July,
I took Samuel Bradley, from Tolland, and told
him the story, and asked his advice. We both
went to see Lavee. I offered to " leave it out"

again to any three persons that he might choose. He said that he would not leave it to God, man, or the devil, and used such language as I never heard before. Bradley then advised me to sue for my pay, as the only possible way of getting anything, especially as my creditors of whom I purchased the machinery, would only wait for their pay on condition of my prosecuting him. I gave the matter into his hands, and he commenced a suit against him, which so enraged him that he undertook to destroy my character in every possible way. He spared no pains nor money to accomplish his hellish purpose. He ransacked both states, Mass. and Ct., and succeeded in getting one of my creditors to *sue me* for the very things I had got for him, Lavee.— This was a *rummy*, by the name of Hovey. He could not get the Trasks, my other creditors, to either sue me or sell the account ; they knew me and were temperance men. He worked among my enemies, the rappers, rummies, and rowdies, to get something against my character to appear against me in court. He also got one of the lowest stamp of lawyers to assist him.— He is considered a disgrace to the profession. After a number of days hard labor, they succeeded in drumming or buying up some half dozen disaffected persons to give in their depositions as to my character, and these all lived in *another town*, they not being able after two or three days' trial to get even one in the village or town where

I had lived for thirty years or more. The depositions are all in being now, and will read as follows. In the main, *First* : I know nothing against Munger myself ; but *some* people don't like him. I should think by what I have heard that his reputation was not good. *Second*—*I* never had any difficulty with Munger, but have often heard him spoken of as not minding his own business ; and character bad. *Third*—I have known Munger many years. I never had any difficulty with *him*, but *he* has had difficulty with *others*. On cross-examination, he said that this difficulty grew from his *prosecuting people*. *Fourth*—Nearly the same. *Fifth*—*I* never had any difficulty with Munger, and thought he was a first rate man, only he put some boys into the " town-pound" for fishing Sunday. This was a foreigner, as well as two of the others.

The next had known nothing against Munger for thirty years. All this did not touch the point desired, and this 200 lb. attorney contended that *he* had a right to testify, and after some questioning with *his* eloquence, he got the privilege, and swore solemnly as near to a lie as he could, and keep his supposed dignity up above ground. The depositions show these facts.

An offset to the above :—I asked some of my neighbors to go before lawyer Whittaker and depose. I didn't tell them what I wanted, and was present only at the taking of only a part of the testimony. The questions were mostly put by Mr. Whittaker, Lavee's *first* attorney or counsellor in this place, Lavee being present with his great intellectual 200 lb. to hear what men would say where I lived.

Testimony of *T. W. Carter, Esq.*, agent of the Armes Manufacturing Company, in Chicopee Falls:—I have known Munger for twenty years or more. His character good as a Christian and mechanic. I think him fully competent to design and get up the machinery for a saw or grist mill.

Testimony of *Otis Chapman, Esq., Paymaster* of the Chicopee Manufacturing Company, alsoa Justice of the peace:—Have known Munger for over twenty years, and never heard his character called in question. I consider him an energetic and thorough business man, and of good repute among us.

Rev. R. K. Bellamy, Baptist minister:—Have known Munger about seven years. Consider him a good Christian and citizen, actuated by correct religious principles. Cross examined:—Do you think his doctrines correct? Ans.—Probably as correct as mine, although we differ in some things.

Ezekiel Blake, agent of the Chicopee Manufacturing Company:—I have known Munger seven years or more, and knowing nothing against him as a Christian or mechanic, have

employed him on our works to my satisfaction.
He is a good mechanic to build either saw mill
or grist mill.   Cross examined :—How do you
know of his competency ?   Ans.—Because he
has erected both, in this place, and they show
for themselves. *John E. Marsh*, Mr. Blake's
foreman in mechanism, testifies to the same
thing in substance.

L. Dickinson, Post-master :—I have known
Munger eighteen years or more, and have lived
near him.   I cannot say anything against his
character as a Christian, and a good citizen.—
Plinny Cadwell, Justice of the peace, testifies
to nearly the same thing.

Jeduthan Gleason testifies :—I have known
Munger from twelve to fifteen years, and know
nothing against his Christian character.   I have
employed him to take charge of planning, building, and starting my grist mill, and have not
been dissatisfied.

Lewis Calkins testifies :—I have known Munger by reputation, twelve or fifteen years, and
been acquainted with him ten or twelve years,
and know that he stands as high as any man
among us, for truth, veracity, and a good Christian character.   I have seen his work on mills,
and I would sooner hire him than any other
man that I know of, to erect a saw, or grist
mill for me.

There are a number of other testimonies of
similar character which I do not mention, for

here is enough to *hang* any man, even if he was *not* guilty. These are witnesses who stand as high in the community as any in the State, and are men who are not identified with me in any way, temporally or spiritually, and came at a moment's notice, without knowing what questions were to be put to them, for I did not consult them. It would have done no good if I had, for they were independent minded men, and the 200 lb. *nothing* found it so, in trying to cross-question some of them. I did not call upon one of my particular friends, nor relations, which are numerous. I thought if the *devil* wanted me to be put to the test, I would stand it, and one of *his* friends said to me, your character stands 100 per cent. better than I expected.

I will now say that I am very much obliged to the friends who so promptly came forward to my help in this time of need and deep trial, caused by the devil and his workmen, and as I have not yet been able to pay you even your traveling fees, if I am prospered, you shall have your reward. Let me here say, that I had no more idea of publishing this circumstance when it happened, than I have now of applying for the president's chair. But I felt it a privilege at least, to let the Cain family know that I shall not dodge into the dark yet.

With these facts, and many others, brought on the stand by the personal appearance of my friends at Tolland, I met the issue after two days' trial. The decision was in my favor, but only a part of my *bill* was allowed. How far *politics*, *rum*, or the *devil* had to do with the decision, I cannot yet tell ; but it was evident that some if not all of these three influences had a finger in the pie. To see the class of evidences arrayed against me, and hear them swear, for some of them did swear to facts, two or three times over, and had to come into court the next day and *retract*, to save being taken for perjury. There was a determination on the part of the "Cain family" to destroy me, and when they were likely to fail in their hellish design, their last resort was to get a *Hide* of some kind and apply to me ; which was ingeniously and maliciously applied in his *plea*. I got a *part* of my case, but lost all that was due me, which was $150. This is the justice in going to law with the "Cain family." This is the first case that I ever had in money matters that went to judge, or jury, for a settlement, and it will be the last. This will come up again I hope, where justice will be done, and the Judge cannot be bribed.

Great credit is due to my attorneys, Messrs. Loomis and Brockway, for the fair and manly course which they took, and I dare here appeal to them for the truth of the statements which I have made. I mean to give battle to these three unclean or wicked spirits to which I

have alluded, and by which I have been so un-
justly injured. But the wicked will not go
unpunished. This is a promise, and vengeance
belongs to God, and he says that he will repay,
and I leave this subject there, and proceed with
a more agreeable subject. With all my temporal troubles, I have endeavored to encourage
others to look beyond this ungodly world for
enjoyment, and thousands know that I have labored the last few years, mostly in other places,
as I feel the words of Christ to be true, where
he says, no prophet or Christian is without
honor save in his own country and in his own
house. This is the reason why I feel that my
weak efforts will do more good in other places,
especially when I have so many pressing invitations to go out from home.

I will now give a synopsis of the lecture which
I delivered against the Rappers in Warwick,
R. I., by a special request from the citizens of
that place. I pen this, because it is the last
one that I delivered up to date, August 6th,
'55, and fresh in my mind.

It appeared by the letter that I received, that
the Rappers had nearly taken the place, for no
one understood their design, and religion was
very low at this time. This new fable was presented as the most holy thing ever yet out.—
They used prayer, and quoted scripture, sung
hymns, &c., all calculated to deceive if possible
the very elect. Many had left their several

churches, and followed this fable. One of the *she* clairvoyants, dared the preacher, or any one else, to open their mouths against them. *This*, and other things, scared some and provoked others. The above is the state in which I found the place when I arrived. There was some anxiety to know whether I would come, or not. Deacon Wait, the man that wrote me the letter, came some eight or ten miles with a team, after me, at the rail-road. Sunday arrived, and when I was attending another appointment some distance off, I was told that the cashier of the bank and another gentleman had come on purpose to see if I was in town. On being told that I was, they desired an interview; it being at noon time, some one pointed me out to them. The man came up and introduced himself, and wanted to know if I was the man that was going to lecture down town at 6 o'clock. I told him that I intended to, if the Lord was willing. He said that he came on purpose to see if I had come, for there was much anxiety on both sides. He said that the Rappers had heard that some one was coming and had been fortified. They had obtained extra help, and had two meetings that day in the house where I was to lecture. He hoped that I should not labor so hard as to make me unable to attend down town. I told him that he must *pray*, for God could do great things. This appeared to be a new idea to him. I found, after they had left, that they were both Universalists. Six o'clock arrived, and the house was full, so that I had to take some of the boys up in the desk with me to make room for the ladies to sit down, so ladies were accommodated and boys kept still. I saw that there was much anxiety. After I got my nerves still, I arose, and commenced as follows :

I suppose that this congregation have come here to hear something about the spirit-rappings, according to notice. I shall use the Scriptures to establish the position that I take. *First*, to show that Rapology is not what it pretends to be. *Second*, to show what it *is*, or what it will be, when the fruit appears. The Rappers pretend to have communications from the same source that the prophets did, for spirits of just men made perfect, are the angels, and all the manifestations were had when the prophets were in vision, or a clairvoyant state, for they were clairvoyants or mediums, through which the spirits communicated, and Job showed that fact. The Witch of Endor was a good medium, and the Revelator said that he had a spiritual communication from one of the prophets, and this communication is recorded in the Bible, as true, and they all pretend to believe it. Now I shall try to disconnect this web of the devil, and show that there is no resemblance between the communication given to the prophets, and that angels are *not* spirits of dead men—Heb. ii : 2. See the account of the first angels, Gen.

iii : 24. Here is a literal work done, and an
effectual one, which was true, and not false.—
There were no mediums, no tables tipped nor
raps heard. Why? because, this is the work
of two angels. By the way, you Rappers, look
at *this* fact, Adam's *spirit* had *not yet departed.*
Where do you get the proof that *spirits* are
made into angels? Not from the Bible, for
this fact alone unhitches *your* old dirt car, and
it will go down grade, to hell, where it belongs.
But I will give you the account of the work of
a few more angels that God created before he
did man on purpose to send on errands of judgment and mercy ; and, according to the text,
their words were steadfast. Gen. xviii : 23.—
These angels said that they were going to destroy
Sodom : Did they tell the truth? See chapter xix : 1, 28, 29, and you will see whether
their words were steadfast or not. Look at the
visit which Gideon, the son of the Abiezrite had
while threshing *wheat,* not in a *clairvoyant
state.* Here was literal conversation, a bargain
closed, a work done, and without any rapping
or table tippings. See Judges vi : 11, 20, 21,
22, and you will be ashamed, if you have any
shame, to *try* to blend this transaction with
your jugglery. But to proceed.—Look at the
visit of an angel to the three worthies in the
midst of the fire. Let us see you come up to
your work, and take one *"sitting,"* in such a
place as that, and if you do not get scorched,

then I will believe. Now see Dan. vi : 22, and
viii : 16, and onward, and hear the angel Gabriel, a servant to Daniel, sent by God, on an
errand, and ix : 21, 22, &c. He comes again,
but no table tippings nor rappings. Now look
at the New Testament, Luke i : 18, 19 ; hear
the same Gabriel saying that he stands in the
presence of God, and is one of God's cabinet,
giving instructions to Zacharias about John the
Baptist's birth, &c. Again, in six months, he
appears to Mary, and tells her about the birth
of Christ. In less than a year he appears unto
the shepherds, and tells them where they can
find the Saviour. There was great rejoicing,
for Gabriel had taken many other angels with
him on this occasion, for it was a great one.—
Now look at *this*, you *green rappers.* The *ripe
rappers* have said in *Chicopee Falls* that this
Christ, who caused so much rejoicing, was
nothing more than a bastard, and I can bring
those who heard them say so. This is one of
the *ripe fruits* of Rapology, and you will find it
so if you go on to perfection in Rapology.—
Look at the visit of an angel to Peter in prison.
See if this transaction agrees with your flat,
sinful, pretended communications. Read the
account, you will find it in the Acts, xii: 7, 8,
9 ; and v: 19. Now bring on your mediums,
and do something worth while ; not sneak
around in the dark, tipping tables and rapping,
and then getting nothing but lies, unless you

happen to guess right occasionally. Don't try
to make this community believe that your communications are from the same source that the
Prophets, Apostles, Gideon, Lot, Mary, and the
shepherds were, for no one who reads their Bible
will believe you. See Rev. xxii: 8 ; here is your
favorite text, to show that the spirit of one of
the Prophets came to John ; but on this, you
are as blind as a beetle. You are willingly deceived, and are deceiving others. Now let us
examine this. Look at the 6th verse, and you
will see that the Lord God of the holy Prophets
sent his *angel*. See 8th verse, and John says
that it was an *angel*, and he fell down to worship him, and the angel said to John, See thou
do it not, for I am only thy *servant*, and (*servant*)
of thy brethren the prophets. See him serving
the three worthies. He told John not to worship him, but God. Now read the 16th verse,
I, Jesus, have sent mine *angel* to testify unto
the church, or John, which is the same thing
here. Now where is your proof that *this* is not
an angel the same as the others. To deny this,
you wrest the scriptures to your own destruc-
tion. I have shown, that your foolish pretended proceedings, bear no resemblance to the posi-
tive, steadfast words and works of the angels.

Of course you are not of that class, and as
you belong somewhere, I will try to find your
proper place, and show you and this congregation where it is. I want you should understand

that I shall be pointed in attacking·this delusion, and whatever I may say, it is not person-
ally applied to any *individual*, for I know not
a person in the house ; you are all strangers to
me, and I want you to be as quiet as possible
while I feel for the main pillars of Rapology,
and if any of you have taken shelter under this
old hovel, that is erected upon the sand, don t .
find fault with me, as having any *personal* difficulty at stake ; it is your *doctrine* that I am
after.   But to proceed.—The doctrine of Rapology is not a *modern* thing, it is as old as *Moses*, and commenced then.   It began to be a
torment to the church *then*, and has been ever
since.   God has, in every age, pronounced a curse
upon this class, and those that consulted them,
instead of the Lord.   You are in very happy
circumstances, compared to your ancestors, who
lived under the Mosaic dispensation, for you
would all be killed, or have to run as your fathers did.   Now I am about to introduce a class
of Scriptures to show what Rapology is, and
track it down from the days of Moses, to the
present day, as clear as a fox was ever tracked
in a new snow ; see Ex. vii : 11, 12.   This
kind of anti-christians was called the wise men
of Egypt by Pharaoh, and they withstood the
children of God, just as you Rappers do, *now*,
in pretending to work *miracles*, as the sorcerers
and magicians did then.   But God's Moses and
Aaron out-did them at last, and liberated his

children from slavery.   Moses was the first *abo-
litionist* that effected the emancipation of his
people ; see Ex. xxii : 18.   Now see how much
God thought of *your* ancestors.   He had seen
their works, and ordered the Israelites to kill
them.   Now read Lev. xix : 31.   God tells his
children not to regard what these ancient Rappers said, and so *I* tell *you ;* see Lev. xx: 6.—
You will now see their character as to *chastity.*
I will notice that again in its place.   Next read
Deut. xviii : 10–15, and you will see the hatred
of the Almighty towards this same class, and
forbidding his people to follow their example
in any way.   Now see if I have done you injustice by classing you with the witches and wizards of olden times, for here is a case in point,
a fac-simile of the Rappers.   Here I intend to
hitch your old dirt car to the right train.   See
1 Sam. xxviii: 6–18.   Here you will see a backslider from God, just as nearly as *all* the Rappers are, after God will not communicate with
them, on account of their wickedness, and like
Saul hunting around after a witch, who pretended to talk *with the dead.*   See now the first
performance of the old rapper with Saul.   After
an introduction, he wanted to ask questions.—
She knew all the while who he was, and had
kept watch of his movements, and his trying to
disguise himself only fitted him the better to be
deceived by her, for you recollect that those persons possessed great wisdom, and you Rappers

brag of *yours*. This old hag knew Saul from his height. For the Bible says that he was a whole head and shoulders taller than any other man in Israel, and it does not look likely that she did not know him, from this fact. Again, she left her former residence, for fear of this same Saul, when he was in favor of God, and obedient to Samuel. He was the very one that threatened her with death. She *did* know him, and knew that he had got away from God, and got over there, and she had a good chance to make herself popular at his expense. Now see the clairvoyant or rapper operate. What do you want, my friend? I want you to raise Samuel to talk with me. This gave the old witch the advantage completely, and she kept it. She then *pretended* everything done, and Saul *saw nothing* himself; all was done through her, after this, for Saul asked, (when *she* pretended to be so *frightened*,) what *she saw?*— *He* saw *nothing ;* and again asked, what *form he was of*. He saw nothing *yet*, nor didn't at all, only believed what the witch told him ; just as the Rappers do now, believe *their* witches. They see nothing themselves, but must believe what the medium says, and this is the very way that Saul perceived that it was *Samuel* speaking to him. See Adam Clarke's comment upon this passage. These witches and wizards had, among the rest of their arts, the art of ventriloquism. *That* was calculated to deceive. This was what Saul heard, and with her knowledge of his affairs, and the backslidden state which she knew that he was in, she could well guess or know what would become of him, and his sons, if the Philistines *did* conquer, which they must, and this is all the knowledge that she had, and she guessed partly right, *that* time, as the mediums do now.

I have not finished yet. Now, if the course of the old witch had *pleased* the Lord, as she pretended to do a part of his work, that is to *raise the dead*, would not mention be made of it in another place, as is the case, for God always kept his books on the principle of double-entry, especially such an important transaction as this. He certainly would, and did ; and you will find it in his *ledger* kept for that purpose, 1 Chron. x : 13, 14. Here you will see that God has not yet changed his course as some have supposed, but dealt with Saul just as he had said he would previously, if any one of his professed followers consulted one of these things. Saul disobeyed the Lord, and the Lord killed him for going over to Endor to consult the old she-rapper ; for she is the first one that we have any particular account of, that pretended to talk with the dead.

Now I think all can see that I have done you no injustice by placing you just where the Scriptures do. This whole affair taken in its connection makes out this fact only—that Saul never saw Samuel, for he never arose. It was all a piece of deception played on Saul at the expense of his character and even his life. And as God has not changed, he will curse all of *you*, if you continue in this ungodly course. I am now talking to professors ; for there are always a class, as scum floating upon the community, that God never mentions, unless they come in contact with his people, as the above. This class may as well be Rappers, as anything else, for they will only be a curse to the community wherever they are ; and this rake of the devil may as well gather them into one " bundle" first as last, " to be burned up," root and branch. But you, oh man of God, flee from these things and turn unto *Him*, and he will pardon you for what little you have been deceived, if you will now hear the truth and obey it. But to return to the subject and follow it down still further. Look at the book of Job, at the place where the Rappers claim that he had a spiritual communication ; see Job iv : from the twelfth verse to the end of the chapter. If you notice it is old *Eliphaz*, Job's *enemies*, or miserable *comforters*, as he calls them. This was an old Rapper who pretended that he had a vision, &c., see 16th verse. He contradicted himself twice, *just* as the Rappers do now. The thing that he saw stood *still ;* but he could see *nothing* of a form, yet it *was an image* that *passed* before his *eyes.* There was perfect *silence,* and yet he *heard* a *voice*, saying, Shall mortal man be more just than God, &c. Now he goes on to tell Job a number of lies. Hear him in the 18th verse telling Job that God puts no trust in his *servants*, and even his *angels* he charged with folly. Now all of this was a *lie*, and does not correspond with God's word anywhere ; and I have been astonished when I have heard old professors and some preachers take this account for the words of *Job*, who was a perfect man of God, when it came from one of his enemies. Now, to show that Eliphaz was a Rapper, look at the 5th chap., 1st verse, and you will see that after he had told all of the above story to Job, he supposed that he was convinced by that time of his talent, and wanted him to call the *spirit* or *saint* that he would like to have *answer him.*— Now, who does not see that this was the work of one of the old Rappers that tormented Father Job in his afflictions ? God condemned their course, and they had to go to Job, and confess their sins, and get Job to pray for them. Now if you Rappers can make anything out of this account to benefit your case, you are welcome to it. The evidence is all against you, just like the case of Saul and the witch. But I shall follow you still further—Isaiah viii : 19, 20. You will see that the people of God are cautioned against your ancestors, and they were told then when they were asked to seek after those that have familiar spirits that peep and mutter, (and rap,) and want the living to go to the dead for light, to go then to the law and testimony, try them, and if they speak not according to that, it is because there is no light in them. This is God's advice, and I have endeavored to follow it, and am after your dark lanterns of iniquity, and in His name I mean to follow up this devil while I remain in the vineyard.

I will now follow your ancestors down into the Christian dispensation. See Paul contending with a false prophet, a sorcerer, whose name was Bar-jesus. He did all that he could to counter-act the work of God done by the Apostles, in turning the deputy from the faith of the Gospel. Paul, being filled with the Holy Ghost, hated them much worse than I do you, who are doing the same work. He himself gave them their true character, " Oh, full of all subtlety and all mis-chief, thou child of the devil, thou enemy of all righteousness, you are perverting the right ways of the Lord ;" and for this Paul pronounced a curse upon him, and God smote him with blindness, which caused the deputy to see the difference between these two powers, and he be-lieved in God, and was steadfast afterwards.— For this fact see Acts xiii : 6–13. Still Paul kept at his work, and more of this same class came in his way, and tried to counterfeit the Word of God, just as the Rappers do now.— These were vagabonds : there were seven of them, and this number made a good *circle*. But the spirit they called up happened to be ugly, just as they are now according to your own admission. This spirit was cross, and said, *Jesus* I know, and *Paul* I know; but who are ye: and the spirit fell upon them, and overcame them, and prevailed against them. Fear fell on all the clairvoyants in that region, and the work of God still went on. You see that I am on your track; for this class always have been opposed to the work of God. It is anti-christ. For the above account, look at Acts xix: 10–18. Still further; you will see in Gal. v: 19–22, the *characteristics* of *ripe* Rappers—fornication, adultery, murder, witchcraft, and many other things classed under the head of the works of the *flesh*. I can *name* some men who are living with other *men's wives at this time*, claiming that it was *directed by the spirits*, and if I should tell one half of the truth about these unchaste anti-christians, called Rappers, you would hide your head. I am told by those that have left them, that one of their great mediums (after they had been led by him for months as "the great power of God") got drunk and swore at a great rate at the spirits for not tipping the table soon enough. Soon after, the spirits dictated him to take a she-clairvoyant for his spiritual wife. They went off together, and I suppose, by reports, that they have got a spiritual baby. Now you delicate rappers here, don't blush at this, for you will soon know of worse things than this if you keep on ; for you are coming on to the ground with Shakers, Mormons and Catholic Priests, in this respect, as well as your other faith, i.e. holding communications with the dead. These are all older children than you are.— Look at your old mother of harlots peeping in- to purgatory to see the *spirits of the dead* and damned, and offering to get them out for so much money. Again, see old Ann Lee, the Shaker. She had spiritual communications.— The Shakers told me that they had commu- nications from her every week. Now see Joe Smith and his followers in the same line, only a little ahead of you, and *all* forbid to mar- ry, but have wives enough, and you are follow- ing in the same spiritual line. I think these institutions are the devil's three-legged stool, and I will warn you to keep clear from the whole concern—in the name of God, keep clear, But lastly, see 2 Tim. iii : 1–9, you will find that in the last days perilous times shall come, and it tells what these perils *consist of, and the worst one is that the same spirit will be revived to withstand the Church down *here*, that with- stood it in the days of *Moses*, that is, by pre- tending to work miracles. The Rappers are the very people that are trying to imitate this thing, as Jannes and Jambres tried to imitate the works of Moses, and the sorcerers tried to imitate Paul. I told you that this was as old as Moses, and have proved it by tracking it

back to where I first started, showing clearly that I have the straight track, for you can
see from one end to the other. I do not pretend to be a prophet or a prophet's son, nor a
preacher or a preacher's son ; but I do profess a
little common sense, and have an interest in this
warfare, and mean to serve the church. If the
gun that I use is not so large as many that are
now lying still, I will load it, and fire the heaviest shot that I can throw, for small shot will not
answer for the devil in these days—he has got
quite too bold under these squibs. I will close
now by saying, I have come over a hundred
miles to attend this appointment, I have spoken
nearly an hour and a half ; you have paid good
attention, and I hope it will be a lasting blessing to *some* of you at least ; and if any of this
class (before mentioned) call upon you to give
heed or hearing to this devilish seducing spirit,
let my last advice be to you, Give it a tremen-
dous letting alone. Amen."

After the exercises closed, there was an offer
made of the town hall for the next evening, which
I accepted. I consented to speak Monday evening on the subject of Practical Christianity,
which I hope was not lost upon the congregation.
It was large and attentive : many appeared serious, and shed tears freely. Thus ended my
first and last visit at that place. I did my duty
as well as I could, and left my skirts clear from

the blood of all in that place, knowing that I should shortly meet them in the Judgment. I arrived at home in season to attend to the duties of the Wilbraham camp-meeting, which commenced August 20, 1855, of which I will not make any record, although it was a good, profitable meeting, like many others that I have attended which I have not named. I have now nearly done with this short and imperfect narration, and if it is the means of any good or light, I shall be glad. I hope that it will not do any hurt, and all the good it does will not atone for any of my sins, and if I am saved, it will be a sinner saved by grace.

I will give a part of a letter received from a member of the church in Warwick, two weeks after the lecture.

WARWICK, *Aug.* 24, '55.

Mr. MUNGER—Dear sir : I will say in regard to your visit to this place, we shall always be very grateful. The Rapping excitement is dead. Their sandy foundation shook, and there are very few now that meet at all. Our church has been much blessed by your coming among us only once. May God bless and sustain you in the labor of his works, and give you a final reward in his kingdom at last. In haste,

J. B. WAIT.

I have many letters similar to the above, but don't consider them worth publishing. Per-

haps one more fact will not be amiss. While
I was on a journey, I stopped at a depot,
when a stranger came to me, and offered his
hand. I told him that I did not recollect him,
but he said that he recollected me, and never
should forget me, and as the cars would not go
under an hour, he wanted me to take dinner at
his expense. I refused, thinking probably, that
this was some one that I had made an impression upon, either by *law* or the *rod*, or some
other unwelcome instrument, as I often met
with such cases. He insisted, and I saw that
he had called for refreshments for two. When
we got through eating, he wished to explain
himself. Said he, do you remember a man that
got up once when you was lecturing and went
out, scolding? I told him that I did not, in
particular, for *that* thing often occurred, especially among the Rappers, but I hoped that
he was not one. He said that he was, at that
time, and he had established a circle in that
place. He had two sittings that Sunday, and
was assembled for the third, when one of his
neighbors told him that there was going to be
a lecture against the Rappers, that evening,
and he (his neighbor) wanted to go, and so did
others. *He* finally suspended his operations,
for two hours, took his mediums and went over
to see if anything could be said against his position, for he had never heard anything *then*, to
weaken his faith in it. Accordingly they all

sat together to strengthen each other, and oppose me, by their concentrated wills. When I got about through, he said that he saw that I had got the ears of the congregation, and some of his anticipated converts. He said that my fifty or sixty passages of Scripture were differently arranged, from anything that he had ever heard, or thought of, and when I called his mediums the descendants of the sorcerers of olden times, and all that consulted them the descendants of that old backslider, Saul, and proved it, and many other hard things, he could not stand it. He went out, and when he got to the head of the stairs, he said that he called me a damned liar, or rascal. When he got down, he saw a number at the foot of the stairs, who heard what he had said, as he left the hall. They knew him, and told him that he had got his match that time, and other things that irritated him. He stayed down stairs until I closed, and when his little flock got together, he dismissed them for *that* time, for he saw that he could do nothing that night. After he got home, he took the Bible and looked over the passages, and found them correct. He then began to reflect, and was converted to the truth of my position, and if he admitted THAT, he must the *rest*. He saw that he was doing the work of the devil, and was in trouble. He tried to pray, and sat up till three o'clock. He became convinced of his wrong, and promised God, that if he would forgive him, he would try to undo what he had done. The next day, he commenced the work, by telling the circle that he was convinced that he, and all the rest, were in the wrong, and God had handled him hard all night. This broke up *that* circle, and many had gone back to their churches, and *he* among the rest. He was that day on his way to meet a circle that he had established, and tell them that God had showed him his wicked course, and to warn them of theirs. He told me that he had every passage of scripture that I quoted with him, and used them. He showed them to me and others, at the time, for there were a number in the saloon when he told this tale. It had a good effect upon some who were leaning towards Rapology. He bade me good bye, and I have since heard that he was a good, devoted Christian.

A few Thoughts on Miscellaneous Subjects.

POLITICS.—This is a subject that I have taken but little interest in for the last twelve years, not enough to go to the ballot-box once in that time. Such a confusion of ideas, and interests to be consulted, took more knowledge than I had to know what *duty* was ; and it certainly had ceased with me to be a privilege to follow the changes caused by office-seekers, having their own interests at stake rather than the good of the people—and the very laws that were made by such mighty efforts, were broken by the very ones who made them. I came to the conclusion to obey, rather than to make them for others to break, which was so fashionable.

FASHION.—This is a very expensive luxury. It costs more to support it than it does the actual necessities of the poor. To keep up with the fashion, it would need something swifter than the express train. Those who have spent all their time and money, after all have not got any thing substantial. It is like reading novels ; the more you read, the less you have : or, in other words, like a " cribbing horse," fill up with wind and grow poor all the time, only creating an appetite for wind, which destroys the digestive organs for solid food.

RICHES.—They are a convenient curse generally. How seldom do you see the rich happy. They are like a troubled sea that casts up mire and dirt, always in a fret to take care of what they have got, and mad because they haven't got more, or show no signs of thankfulness 'for what they have got. They go through life on a gallop, to run away from the foolish poor who are chasing them up, with appearances only.— This puts me in mind of two sheep that I had the care of. One, in trying to get out of the pasture, fell into the mud and disfigured himself. This disgusted the other that had the clean coat, so he ran to keep out of the way.—

The dirty one, not seeing his own situation, gave chase to gain the company of the other, and both ran themselves nearly to death. Riches generally prove a curse to those who have them, and the poor who are so foolish as to covet them, commonly imitate the rich in appearance.— This curse follows the next generation. How seldom do you see the rich man's sons make good citizens. They are generally indolent, extravagant, intemperate, and wicked, setting bad examples to all around them, and often spend what their parents left them, and many times come to *want* before the eyes of their parents, if they are not degraded and loaded with crime. Look into the halls of legislation, and see how few you find there of rich parentage. Look into the former and present battle fields, and see who have gained our liberties, and yet maintain them. Look into the different departments of industry and improvement, and see where the acknowledged intellectual strength that this country boasts of, comes from. Not from the sons of rich men. Look into the ministry, and see who you will find. You will not find the sons of rich men *there* half so often as you will in the jail, penitentiary, or on the gallows. These are facts, that I have observed, and I envy not the rich, for their troubles are double the honest poor man's, who has struggled with poverty, brought up a large family of children, and educated them in the school of economy and good morals, and

in his old age can look back with pleasure upon
his children, who are winding their way into influence, gained by their own hand of industry and perseverance, becoming the bone and
sinew of the country, knowing quite well what
money and character costs. These men make
the good financiers, prudent in all things. while
obedient and trustworthy. This is generally the
case with the sons of poor men. They have
been trained up in the way that they should go,
while, on the other hand, the sons of the rich
have always been dandled upon the knee of in-
dulgence, and if they ever do get an office, it is
not because they have merited it by their industry and good morals ; but it is because they
have had friends of influence that have pushed
them into office. This accounts for so many
public spendthrifts in the land—they have never
learned the first great lessons of industry and
prudence.

POVERTY.—This, I am familiar with. I began with nothing, and have held my own very
well. I have found out that the way to enjoy
myself in poverty, is not to let my wants run
ahead of my means. A man's wants need bri-
dling, or cultivating. The actual wants of a
man are very small. Let him buy nothing that
he can do without, and *save* every thing that is
worth saving, and that will be every thing that
is worth making, or raising, even to a pin, a
nail, or a kernel of corn. A penny saved is

worth more than one earned by ten per cent ;
for if you save it, you *have* it, but if you earn
it, you must collect it, and in these days many
are glad to get off by discounting ten or twenty
per cent. to *have* their earnings collected.—
There are many unnecessarily poor, on account
of getting their head forward of their heels in
the first start.   They let their wants take the
lead, and try their credit, and wear it out, and
for years go bent over, scolding and muttering
and annoying every body that is better off than
themselves, when in fact they have had the same
or a better chance than the ones that they are
muttering about, and in reality this difference
in their situations was caused by the following
course : one let his wants run away with his
means to keep up appearances, and by so doing,
wore poor credit out in its youth : the other
studied economy as well as fashion, saved as well
as earned, and never *promised* to pay, without
a good probability of doing so at the time. Poverty is a virtue connected with honesty and economy, while riches are a curse without them.—
There are said to be three kinds of poor : 1st,
the Lord's poor—2nd, the devil's poor—and 3rd,
poor devils.   The first class of poor will serve
God contented with their lot, and are always
ready to contribute something to benefit others,
if it is not silver or gold.   It will be helping
such as want help in sickness and distress, or
trouble.   This kind of help is often the best ap-

preciated, and does more good than money.—
See the Apostle's great gift—Silver and gold
have I none ; but such as I have give I unto
thee. The second class of poor are those who
serve the devil in their poverty, and make everybody miserable around them, (dumb beasts not
excepted.) Everything goes wrong : if they are
at a boarding house, they will find fault with
the board, and want a great deal of partiality
shown them, and they will generally run away
and not pay for their board. This class is getting to be very common. The third class are
those who are well off as to money, but put it
to such uses as to spread devastation and ruin
in their path. If they give at all, it will be
where it will be a curse to the community, like
helping the convict that ought to be shut up for
his crimes, to escape justice, and continually
scattering firebrands in the community, like
burning buildings, seduction, theft, drunkenness,
robbery, murder, &c. Many of this class have
escaped justice, through the influence of money
paid by this class until their money is all gone,
and when this is the case, you will see very
plainly that they are left to be poor devils. For
when their *money* is gone *all* is gone, and they
lost it by serving the devil. Poor devils truly !

A WORD ON LAW.—There are more kinds of
law than poverty, and resorts to law to get our
dues generally lead to poverty or perplexity, at
least. I shall not undertake to justify nor con-

demn others for using the *law. I will only
here introduce the opinion that I had formed a
few years ago. After looking the subject over,
I published the following article :

APPEALING TO CÆSAR.

Bro. Himes :—As there is such a variety of
opinions concerning the law of our land and the
use of it, it has become difficult or impossible to
have all suited. Some think to use laws in any
case is sin ; others that it is right to make and
use them. Now, with my experience in camp
and other meetings, it's my opinion that it is not
sin to use the law prudently on the lawless and
disobedient. Paul says it was made for such.
He himself applied a number of times to get
justice ; he once obtained the assistance of a
large number of armed men to protect him from
a wicked rabble that sought to injure him ?—
Why not suffer them to kill him ? Because he
thought God had given him a work to do, and
the law would protect him in some measure to
do it ; and he at certain times took advantage
of it, for the sake of preaching the truth to others, which he could not have done, if he had not
used his common sense to save himself. This
was not lifting the sword as some would argue—
no brother going to law with brother. Our
Lord instructed us to watch, and not let the
thief come in and steal or break up our house,

and calls him a good man who keeps him out.
Some of our late reasoners would say that he is
wicked to resist, and should take joyfully the
spoiling of his goods, &c. So I say, when you
cannot help it. But help it when you can, and
not lift the sword. I should think it justifiable,
if he did get my goods, to complain to Cæsar,
and let him take care of him, and not feel guilty
of going to law with my brother either. I claim
no relation to such—he belongs to the *other*
family. Our Lord seemed to take this view of
it at one time. He commenced whipping the
other family, who were intruders, out of the
meeting-house, or temple. I believe it was before the meeting began, and his first public
meeting too. Why not take joyfully the spoiling or defiling the goods or temple? Let our
remarkable docile brethren answer and love
them, if they can.

I will not be hypocritical : I do not love the
devil, neither his works, nor workmen. God
does not require it, and I am glad of it. We
are to be separate until we see signs of repent-
ance. I do not mean to hate them, nor try to
injure them by lifting up the sword ; but to
shun their company, and let them know why I
do so. I have none of this mock charity that
will hug the devil. The most Scriptural bene-
volence that can be shown to an ungodly dis-
turber of your peace is, to let him know how
you view him, in the light of God's word. I

must do it, and if I pray for them appropriately, it is for God to torment them day and night while they remain in their wicked, rebellious course against God and his children.

In many cases, feigned love and idle praying for the conversion of the ungodly, have failed for years ; for God does not convert until the sinner's way is hedged up, and he feels the sorrows of a guilty conscience. The sooner, therefore, this is brought about, the sooner we have the first evidence of a reformation. This is what I call love to the sinner, as much as it is to a child to use the rod in season to save it. To let the, children disturb our family peace, turn things upside down, drive us out of the house that we have procured for our benefit and theirs, is like letting the wicked rabble come in, and disturb, and insult, and undo what God has told us to do, without our taking any steps to prevent it. Order is heaven's first law ; and those that have none and want none, let them enjoy it ; but for the Lord's sake, let those that have maintain it.

I have not written these things for a standard for others ; but the position I have providentially been called to occupy in our public meetings, has placed me in very trying circumstances, some wanting order that they might be benefitted by the meeting they had made such sacrifices to attend ; while others believed in the non-resistant plan wholly, and others, in part.

Such a state of feeling among the brethren exists at present, and what must be done? I ask to be excused for taking the burden of camp-meetings anywhere, unless order can be preserved. The non-resistant brethren, I find, are as glad to enjoy a peaceable time as any one else ; but some of them will resist all lawful measures to bring it about. The Wilbraham meeting for two years has spoken loudly in favor of camp-meetings ; even the papers of different States have noticed our good order and preaching at that meeting ; which would have been lost had the non-resistant principle been acted on.

We only ask Cæsar to take care of his own while we did our work. This, I think, was using the law prudently. Some are so lavish or imprudent in using the law or anything else, that they ought to be non-resistant ; for God has not assigned them that portion of the work—see Rom. xii : 4-8. Many such passages might be found : but I leave the subject for brethren who are capable of doing it justice. No one is responsible for this but myself. I do not expect that all will agree with me, especially those who are so very non-resistant as to invite the wicked to do their worst, and in effect say, " We will bear it all and pray for you." I have seen this done of late, and when the disturbance got at the height, these brethren were among the missing, leaving the rest to suffer on account of their invitations to the wicked to try their courage

and grace, when in fact they had not enough of
either to stand the trial they had provoked.

                              H. MUNGER.
Chicopee Falls, Sept. 11, '50.

Perhaps some may say that I tolerated fighting.   This is a mistake.   In all the difficult and
dangerous places that I have been in, I never
took anything to defend myself with, not even
a stick.   I never have struck a man, in anger,
since I was of age, except Philips before mentioned, and that was necessary to save Hubbard's
life : I have always found some other way better.
I never believed in fighting for peace ; but to
hand over the lawless and disobedient for Cæsar
to govern : I never considered it wrong, if prudence and wisdom were used.   I do not claim
infallibility, and have probably done a great
many things that others have thought wrong ;
but few know what trials I have been through.
Had they been placed in my situation, perhaps
they would have done better ; but God is merciful and wise enough to make allowance for
weak human nature.

After *Law* comes Gospel, and in this subject
I am much more interested than in either of
the others to which I have alluded.   I have
changed some of my opinions on Bible subjects
within the past few years ; or rather I have
tried to search the scriptures for myself; for
before, like many professing Christians, I be-

lieved what men said was true to some extent,
instead of searching the scriptures to see what
God had spoken. Consequently light has broken in upon my mind.

If any body wishes to call me a turn-coat for
this, all I have to say is that *Paul* was a turn-
coat when he quit persecuting the church and
went to preaching Christ, and if any man is
foolish enough to wear his coat wrong side out
for fear that he will be called a turn-coat, he
can do so, but I shan't.

I find out however, that much which I supposed to be *new*, turns out to be old truth,
taught in all the purest ages of Christianity,
believed by all the reformers and by the founders
of the purest churches, and it is still held by
many of the more intelligent in all denominations. So that while many professors of religion suppose that they have the truth and are
walking in the old paths, they have not only
departed from the faith of the Bible, and the
faith of primitive Christians, but also from the
faith of their own founders and teachers.—In
proof of this I shall offer some quotations, mostly from a valuable book entitled "The Voice of
the Church on the Coming and Kingdom of
the Redeemer, or a History of the Doctrine of
the Reign of Christ on Earth," by D. T. Taylor,
which is published by H. L. Hastings : and
those who wish to investigate the matter fully,
are referred to that work. I shall proceed to

give a synopsis of some of my views. On many points, as the belief of the scriptures, the work of conversion, and many others, I need not speak, for I agree doubtless with nearly every Christian reader in those matters, but in some other respects we differ ; and in these respects I claim to be agreed, in some cases, with *all* ancient Christian writers of note, and in other cases with *many* who are well known and honored in the Church of Jesus Christ. I find, however, that *now*, as in years past, it requires some courage and determination to believe and *speak* the truth. Many dare not investigate, and many *more* believe, but *dare not speak* the everlasting Gospel of God. For my part, I wish to adhere to the Old Standards. I am glad that I agree in my faith with so many that are called " Fathers" in the Church, and especially with the " *Grandfathers,*" the *apostles* of the Lamb !

APPENDIX.

As the demands call for a second edition of this book, I think it in keeping with the narrative to give a further account of some of my labors down to the present time.

Before I do this, I will relate the experience of some of our ministers in the opposition which they met while preaching the gospel as it is in Christ, related to me by one who was the principal persecutor in the affair.

For obvious reasons, I withhold the name and place, but will give the substance as near as I can relate.

When the doctrine was being first preached in the town of ——, Conn., the churches there violently opposed it, and said many hard things, and one man, more zealous than the rest, suggested what ought to be done with those who preached it. This man, ready to do any thing to serve the church in putting the error down, commenced by going to meeting to disturb and scoff. But the work of God went on ; souls were converted in spite of his opposi-

tion.   He being enraged and driven on by the
professors of religion, determined to use violent means.   He gathered a company of rowdies, and headed them, for the purpose of
taking the preacher, Brother S. G. Mathewson,
out of the meeting.   The ringleader went first
into the house; but God's power was there,
and he was scared, and retreated precipitately.
Not being satisfied, others tried; but God de-
fended his own truth, and no man dared to
lay hands upon his minister.   This red-hot
opposer told me afterwards that he never saw
a man that he was afraid of before.   He said,
when the preacher looked at him he trembled
and left the house, swearing and much dissatisfied.

The Methodist class-leader put them up to
try once more; but they dared not go in again.
The meetings went on, and opposition raged.
This man told me that, as he got headed in taking Brother Mathewson, he, with others, undertook to stop his going to his next appointment.
They took his wagon to pieces, and carried the
wheels in different directions, some to the
mountains, and others rolled theirs into a
pond.   They got a little victory, as they supposed; but the triumph of the wicked was
short, for Brother Mathewson got another
wagon and went to his appointment, leaving
his case in the hands of God, expecting his
wagon would be in order for him when he re-

turned. I think this man told me that Brother
Mathewson prayed to that effect. But he
thought God would not answer that time, for
no one knew where all the parts were. But
that night he said the wagon haunted him. He
would swear about the Millerites, but could
not sleep. He at length had to go to work to
hunt up the fragments, and got others to help;
but they could not find one of the wheels; on
inquiring diligently, however, they found it
was rolled into the pond; and he, having the
honor of being captain, had the pleasure (?)
of wading in and getting it out. He got it
together, swearing and working and wishing
the devil had them wagon and all. Besides,
on looking it over, he discovered the linchpins
were missing; and although tired and mad he
commenced hunting them up. He found some
of them, others he had to get made. When
the job was completed he damned the wagon
and left it ready for use when Brother Mathewson returned.

Still mad because he had not accomplished
what the church expected, he being such a
bravo, he tried other ways to drive the preacher
out of town. The battle waxed hot. Brother
Baker told me that he had been taken while
praying, and pounded and dragged round the
room, over benches and out of doors, and
kicked until others thought him dead. But
the work of the Lord went on. Some of the

scoffers were smitten by the power of God whilst out of doors, and cried for mercy; some were struck down in the field, some in the road, half a mile from the meeting, and were picked up and carried back by their own request, and converted. God heard prayer and stood by his people. The devil lost ground every step in this persecution, which first started with professors of religion, whose names might here be given. These brethren, as well as those in other places, know something of opposition and persecution in the nineteenth century (1843–44), caused by professed followers of Christ.

But to return to the subject of this man's persecuting spirit. After he had got headed off in mobbing preachers, and unjointing wagons, and many other bad things, he concluded not to go in company with others, but alone, for he was determined to follow up the Millerites, as he called them. He told me he wanted to fight them, but dared not touch Mathewson. On hearing that a man by the name of Hastings was going to preach in the neighborhood, he went to see him. Hastings came late, and requested the brethren to commence the meeting while he was at supper, which he took in his hand and ate in the room, the service going on, and he occasionally saying " amen," etc. This being out of the common order of things, attracted the man's attention so that he kept quiet. When the preacher had finished eating, he knelt down and commenced praying in such a strange way that it stirred him up. He was first astonished, next pleased, then *scared*, for the power God was present. He could not well get out, and so stayed through the preaching, which was as strange as the praying. All served to stir the devil in him

When the meeting was out, the brethren all seemed very anxious to shake hands with Hastings, while *he* felt more like knocking him down. Soon Hastings came to him and passed the compliment, but he swore at him. Hastings shouted; this he took as an insult, and swore again, threatening to whip him, which only made Hastings shout the louder and come the nearer to him. The fellow backed off, threatening and swearing, Hastings following, shouting. He backed out of doors and ran, Hastings after him, crying to God to take him. The fellow jumped the wall, and Hastings kept up till he was so frightened that he ran for home across lots, thinking Hastings was just behind. He jumped fences, brook, and ditches, while those awful words rang in his ears, " God Almighty, catch him ! " On arriving at home, he did not stop for ceremonies, but burst into the house, and ordered his wife to fasten the door. She asked him what was the matter. He said that damned

Millerite Hastings was after him. He jumped into bed just as he was, all in a tremble, expecting to see Hastings come in after him, for he supposed him close behind, which was only imagination, for Hastings did not follow him any distance; but God pursued him by his Spirit. This learnt him the fact that " one could chase a thousand; " for he said afterwards that if he had had a thousand men with him, he should not have dared to face that preacher. This ended his captainship in persecuting the people of God, for, like Saul, he found more than his match to contend with, when his Maker interfered. Soon after this he was converted, and, like Saul, has since shared his part with this people in their rejoicing, in their hope, their suffering and persecution.

The above facts are but a fair sample of what some of us have passed through; they have been related to me a number of times by the man himself, as I generally make his house my home when I am in the place. If any one doubts these facts let him call on John F. Baker, and Rufus Whitehead, in West Winsted, Conn., and he will find that this is only a synopsis of what they will tell him they have witnessed and suffered in the way of opposition and persecution, caused mostly by professors of religion. But God occasionally makes an example, as in the above cases, to show which side he is on. Do you think we have reason to believe that professors are eating and drinking with the drunken, and joining hands with the wicked? Much more might be said about our trials as a people; but we expect to suffer with Christ if we would reign with him, and from the same characters as he did; namely, a cruel, backslidden church, which incited the wicked to serve their master, the devil. What other conclusion can we come to? The fancy, foppish, time-serving professors will shun these things and miss of the kingdom. God has said, If you will live godly, you shall suffer persecution. I don't expect to see even the majority of professors loving the appearing of Christ, or even believing in it, or seeing the signs of his coming. The Scriptures cannot be broken. The wicked will do wickedly, and none of them shall understand. The wheat and tares will grow together till the harvest or end of the world. Christ has said it, and we believe it.

Brother King S. Hastings will be long remembered by me and thousands of others, who claim him as our spiritual father; for he was noted for his zeal and untiring effort; working in every possible way to save sinners, sparing neither time, money, nor reputation, nor even health and life, for he wore himself out in the cause, and died at the age of forty-eight, in peace and triumph over the fear of death, fully believing that the next thing he should know would be to hear the voice of the archangel and the trump of God, calling him from the grave, to shout victory over it, and to enjoy that eternal life which he had so justly earned by complying with the claims of the gospel, which are patient continuance in well-doing. He went by the name of Father Hastings. All who knew him felt a great loss when he died; I in particular, as we were about the same age, belonged to the same church, labored together at camp-meeting among the Methodists, embraced the Advent doctrine together, and I hope shall live together on the new earth. Some of his posterity are left to keep him in remembrance before his many friends.

HIGHWAYS AND HEDGES.

In beginning my labors for the present year, I thought it best to deviate from the beaten track, — this working the old, worn-out fields over and over again, — therefore, I went into Maine and came to South Berwick. I was convinced of the correctness of my conclusion, when I arrived here, finding twenty-one young men all enjoying religion, and five or six young ladies, from my weak efforts here last fall, when I spent only five days. I sowed the seed in what was considered to be a hedge of thorns even by the preacher. On coming home one Friday evening I was happily disappointed to see the seed had taken root and the work had started.

Nine requested prayers the last evening, and I left for Portland, and heard nothing definite from here until I came back this week, when I was greeted with some twenty-five warm-hearted converts I never recollected seeing before. This took me down, as stout as I was, coming so unexpectedly. They all knew me, but I could only say, " What has God done to this thorny hedge ? " I could hardly believe that God had given such increase to so little poor seed. Said one of the church members to me, " We were dead enough to bury when you came last fall." Another said, " I held you off because you were an Adventist, till God broke down my son ; and that showed me that I was fighting God's work ; I broke down and am there yet. Thank God ! " Another said, " I did not mean to get caught as my three brothers did, and so I laid on the floor under one of the back seats to hide from you. But oh ! God took me in hand that night after you had gone, and I had my case to plead alone out in the barn before God." There were other similar accounts of the work of God. This cheered my heart to go into the hedges and work occasionally. This work has spread into the next neighborhood, and many have been converted there. I heard that six requested prayers here the seventeenth.

Sunday. — Although stormy, a good congregation came out through snowdrifts and storm, and four different preachers, to hear the doctrine of life through Christ, and on prophecy, which I had liberty in delivering with very little opposition. None seemed to be bitterly opposed; the converts all drank it down, and now love Christ's appearing. I found only two or three that got their corns trod on hard enough to growl out aloud, and they were barefooted Christians. I advised such to get shod with the preparation of the gospel of peace, for these shoes do not pinch the feet, and will cure these kind of corns.

Wednesday, 22*d.*— The work increases. Last evening nineteen new cases were forward for prayers — some heads of families; a deep feeling prevails in town. Three meetings to-day, and but little work done on the farms; seven different preachers out yesterday.

23*d.* — A good number have come out clear and happy, and others are coming forward. The family where I board have all lately enlisted in the cause of God; four of them within four days. It did look blessed to see seven of them on their knees for the first time.

24*th.* — The interest is increasing. Yesterday, although stormy, as it has been every day since I have been here, the people turned out; some came five miles on foot, and others on sleds drawn by oxen, bringing their dinner and staying all day and evening. A good number were converted, and in the evening some fifteen new cases, and some hard ones. The church has got to work for sinners.

Yesterday, after preaching, forty-two spoke in as many minutes. Last evening the interest was still increasing. There has not been a dog to move his tongue for two days. The first three days there was some grumbling because I broke so many rum-jugs, so one man told me. I find the new wine of the kingdom will burst old rum bottles and jugs, and according to report, quite a number of rum-jugs are in mourning for absent friends. I told the people they must not soak the seed in new rum. Brother Hall, the former pastor, was rejected, I understand, for preaching against rum-drinking, which was practised by many of the members. The old rum-shop now stands within a few feet of the meeting-house; it was built and set in operation by the first pastor, a good, old-fashioned man, that did not think it sin to sell spirits, until he had a dream, and then sold out to the deacon. Such an operation as this would lead to rum-drinking in the church, they being anxious to trade with their own members, and keep their money in the church. This old church rum-shop does not go now, but it has left its effects behind on the inhabitants. Such a state of things was rather forbidding to a protracted meeting, and for a stranger; but so

it was. The preacher that invited me said it
was a Sodom, but he did not go into particulars ; if he had, I should not have undertaken
the job. I begin to see why there were such
sore feet and heads about my preaching.
Surely, it can be called a thorny hedge ; and
nothing but the power of the Almighty God
could ever revolutionize this place. The first
pastor heard of the work, and came nine miles
to see for himself. He staid five days and
helped what he could ; being infirm could do
but little, but did not stand in the way. He
enjoyed to see this work go after so long a
drought. Brother Hall, who lives in this neighborhood, has taken hold with me and rendered
much service, although some rejected him because he came out so strong on rum-drinking ;
but God stands by him.

Saturday, 25th. — Leave to-day for Portsmouth after nine days' meeting. Some fifty
different persons have started anew to serve
God. I left the meeting last evening with
eighteen new cases on their knees pleading for
mercy. The interest has not abated. One
brother said some of the hardest cases in town
were among the eighteen on Friday evening ;
but I was sick and had to leave as soon as I
called them forward. I understand this morning that a number came out blessed. Two men
and their wives resolved to serve God, and
came to the anxious-seats together. One of the

selectmen of the town is among the best labor-
ers, since God's spirit has melted him.   His
family have been blessed by it, and one man
said as I was coming away, " What has God
done for Berwick!   I cannot realize it yet."
And another said, " This crooked people needed
a crooked instrument to hit them."   Consider
the crooked work of God.   Eccl. 7 : 13.   I
think Satan and his workmen will have a job
to straighten things again in Berwick.

This work started as all others do when the
church gets into working order, and it cannot
before.   The preacher can only preach the
people up to their duty of the *Cross*, and then
it will stop until the cross is taken up by those
that have it.   God lays the right cross on the
right ones, and if they refuse to do that duty
they will stop the work, and die themselves.   No
church need to expect a preacher to drive sinners over them; yet many block the wheels,
then find fault with the preacher.

NOTES BY THE WAY.

AFTER leaving the Boston conference, I went
to Portsmouth.   Had a good time.   The Spirit
of the Lord was present to help.   Four young
men and two ladies started in good earnest to
serve God.   From there went to Barnstead.
Found a little company, hated and persecuted

by a formal church, watching every opportunity
to destroy their influence and get their converts away. This made me think of that person who stole a child from its mother and stood
a trial before King Solomon, and lost her case.
The time is soon coming when justice will be
done by our King, and the barren will be
robbed of her stolen children. Thanks be to
God. This meeting resulted in deepening the
work of grace in the hearts of his people. A
number started anew. Some came in from
other towns and lent a helping hand.

Two men from West Clifton, twenty-six miles,
and one from Ossipee Pocket, thirty-eight miles
in the mud, came to hear this blessed truth.
This shows how they love the gospel of the
kingdom who are deprived of hearing it at
home. This brother said he had his sack full,
and it would last him forty days. He went
home rejoicing in the blessed hope.

Although the circumstances were very forbidding, we gained a great victory the last
evening, and left for Loudon Ridge. Here
things looked still more forbidding; a division
of feeling; a small congregation, and bad
weather, and but few to take a part in meeting.
Was most discouraged. Sunday preached on
life through Christ. Some were scared, others
grew mad, a few took courage, and we concluded to hold a meeting Monday evening at
Brother Batchelder's house. I took up the

subject of worldly wisdom in the things of God
as found in 1 Cor. 2d chapter. Had a good
time. Brethren Leavitt and Batchelder backed
it up. The work started a little. Appointed
another on Tuesday evening. Spoke on the ne-
cessity of confessing from the heart. God sent
the word home, and the confession commenced
at nine o'clock and lasted until nearly two the
next morning. It appears that three young
men had covenanted together to brace themselves against any thing that could be said
by any one to them, even had an answer prepared for me if I ventured to speak to them on
the subject of religion. They had their lesson learned and followed up the meetings, ap-
parently secure, occasionally whispering and
laughing. I reproved some of them publicly,
not knowing their design. Tuesday evening
they came again,—that was my last meeting,—
stubborn, and determined to resist every thing
said. At the close of preaching, the brethren
and sisters took hold well. God's Spirit was
manifest. Confession commenced with them.
A backslider confessed, much affected, from ten
to fifteen minutes, then desired prayers. This
rolled the burden and cry on to the church.

The battle began to wax hot, and all had a
spirit of prayer for these three young men, and
commenced praying for them, some five or
six at a time. God heard. They felt; one
ran into the parlor, but it was of no use. When

we all got hold together, God's power came down and prostrated the whole three of them. The one in the parlor cried the loudest for mercy. They remained on the floor over four hours, pleading for mercy and confessing their sins. One, the ringleader, confessed every thing. Said he, "O God! I little thought of this when I came to meeting. I thought I could stand any thing, but this is too much for me." Then they would plead for mercy. We all lost our burden when God rolled it on to them. I went to bed about one o'clock, leaving them on the floor unable to get up. They were left alone to work out their own salvation, which they did about two o'clock in the morning by submitting to God. As one of them was Brother Batchelder's oldest son, where I boarded, he took the other two prisoners of hope into his bed, well satisfied that God was too much for them. They were tame the next morning. All attended prayers, and prayed with us, showing a determination to do their duty, and if they do they will live.

This is the old-fashioned work of God. The world don't know any thing about it; it is hid from the vain and the proud. One old hoper called it excitement; but the more candid neighbor said it was something more than excitement that brought those tears and cries. To-day there is a stir in the place, and I have agreed to stop and hold one more meeting with them.

Wednesday, 19*th.* — Another meeting. The people came from miles around. It went in power. Those three converts took hold of the cross and were blessed, warning their friends with tears to come to Christ. Some were so convicted they left the house ; others requested prayers. After meeting, one of these young men felt it his duty to start on a mission at ten at night to see the one that left the meeting. He went. The man was in bed, but got up and opened the door, and seeing who it was, jumped into bed again. But God had called for him. The young man commenced to pray for him in the dark. God heard prayer, and the man arose again and prayed for himself. So God is doing his own work in his own way.

I left for my next appointment in Portland, ninety-eight miles. There are a few tried friends struggling against the popular current of worldly professors, but they say nothing has hurt them so much as a late thunder-clap from one from whom they should have thought better things.

From there went to Yarmouth, Friday, for a four days' meeting. Found Brother York at the depot waiting, in good spirits. First meeting, one requested prayers, and was blessed.

Saturday. — Two meetings, with more interest. A teacher of the languages came in to hear the preacher, and to criticise ; but it appeared criticism gave way to a powerful convic-

tion which he carried home with him. Sunday
he travelled the lots, mourned and sighed and
prayed, but got no relief. He, knowing Brother
York, sought an interview with him, told him
his feelings; his father was a rich sea-captain and
a professor of religion, and he a teacher in the
Academy. It was a great cross to come to the
Advent meeting to hear my language — it was
not Greek. But Sunday eve he came, not to
criticise on the proper use of language, but to
ask for prayers. When I gave the invitation, he
was the first that arose, to the astonishment of
many present that knew him. Among the
others, a female teacher in the Academy arose
for prayers. After prayers, this young man
prayed for himself, and spoke of his determination to be faithful, although he was placed in
peculiar circumstances, and requested prayers,
that he might be able to go through the opposition that he saw ahead if he should do his duty.
He has just been over to see me. This is the
first time I have spoken to him. He has come
out clear in his mind. Says he took up his
cross this morning, and prayed with the family
for the first time. The family were astonished
to see and hear him pray, having been such a
hard case. He said that he had just told his
mother that he had been to the Advent meeting the evening before and asked for prayers,
and God had heard and blessed him, and he
had started to serve God for life. This was a

new thing. He was asked, " Are you going to be an Adventist ? " " I am going to be a Bible Christian," said he. He asked many questions on experience and doctrine, which I answered. He left to attend his class.

Truly this looks like God's work upon Paul. Imagine my surprise when Brother York told me he was a teacher of the languages in the academy ; but I thought I knew the language of Canaan, and was willing to instruct him what I could. Afternoon meeting, ten prayers in twenty minutes ; fifteen spoke in thirty minutes. This man prayed and spoke, and told what a change had taken place in his mind in two days. One person said, her daughter came home saying there was a great change in her teacher, and the whole school noticed it. God is at work in the academy.

5 o'clock P.M. — More good news. A teacher in the Latin school has just been to see me, and wants to know what she must do to be saved. She is under the cross, deeply convictde. The battle waxes hot just now ; the old church fighting, sinners crying, and we are praying.

Tuesday. — Our meeting last evening result- ed in a victory. The two school teachers took up their cross boldly before their associates and scholars, which had a good effect upon the con- gregation. Some of the scholars wept, the rap- pers looked serious, and one Universalist said it was an interesting meeting. God's Spirit shook the hearts of all present. The threatening of the Pharisees to cast out of the synagogue, did not prevent their hungry sheep from leaping over the bars into better feed. Some said they had been feeding on husks long enough, and they would go where God fed his people. After the meeting was out, one sinner broke down, and we tarried to pray. God answered prayer and she went home happy. I had the pleasure of hearing the school-teacher pray this morning. She has just gone to her school. I hope and expect she will live and teach her pupils more than one lesson. She left saying, "Pray for me, that God will direct me;" the tears starting.

But the time of my departure is at hand. I must soon take Nahum's last day chariots and go to my next appointment. Oh! I am glad there is a gathering-day promised to God's children.

In corroboration of the above I will here give extracts from the letters of Brother R. R. York, pastor of the church in Yarmouth.

YARMOUTH, April 27, 1860.

Dear Brother Hiram, — The battle goes well, bless God. Some new ones started Tuesday evening. The converts appear well. All sorts of lies are in circulation about us, but we know it is false, and it is for Jesus' sake, so on we will go. Our young "college convert" has been to see me twice since you left. He is strong for one so young in the cause. One seeker after Jesus came to our house last evening, and appeared earnest and decided to go ahead. One of those "twin chickens" did a good thing Tuesday evening. After meeting she went to tarry over night at the house of the man for whom you prayed, that God would convert him or kill him dead. While there he gave the meeting a hard run. Little Sis, and others, went to singing a hymn ; this only stirred him up more than ever. She then dropped on her knees and went to praying earnestly, at which he was confounded and said no more. I think he has got a hard row to hoe if he does not submit to God.

To-night we have another meeting. Expect it will be a good one. God bless you, Brother Munger. Rachel is here. They are fighting her hard. Pray for us all.

Yours, in love,   REUFUS.

YARMOUTH, Me., May 25, 1860.

Dear Brother Hiram, — Perhaps you will think I have forgotten my promise to write to you ; but no, I remember it still, and now will give you a short epistle. I should have written before, but our mother, at our house, has sickened and died, which has taken up much of my time. We are still moving on in the path of the just, I trust. Meetings good, and well attended. The converts appear well, and the church generally is awake. Persecution is raging strong, no mistake. The case of the "college brother" excites a great deal of attention. They have almost killed him, but bless God he has revived, as Paul did, when stoned and left for dead. He is strong, and is to be baptized the first Sunday in June. He is a chosen vessel, I trust, for God to use in his vineyard. He is humble and devoted, and says he only wants a chance to get at the people, when he will give them a "thus saith the Lord" for his course. Rachel, "the female teacher," is yet in doubt, and will be till she goes forward. I think she will go ahead yet. The husband of one of those Cumberland sisters has been converted, and is good, bless God. Among the many things we have to meet is the prayer you offered for the husband of Sister Simons. You will remember how you prayed that God would "convert or kill him." Strange to say, he is in all probability dead. He left home last Sunday in a small boat, to go a few miles, and has not returned. All think he is drowned.* This stirs up the people about that

---

* The wretched man was then dead, having been drowned, as was supposed. "'Tis a fearful thing to fall into the hands of the living God."

prayer, but it is all turning against them, for we tell them that
if the man is lost on account of your prayer, they had better
look out for themselves, for God hears prayer. So you see,
that although you have *made work for me*, we have a tremen-
dous power against them. Some say I ought to be hung, others, taken care of; but I am full of courage, glory to God. I
go forth and hold up my head, and have no fear. I believe I
could walk up to the stake for Jesus' sake, if necessary. The
devil is stirring up his subjects, and, bless God, the saints are
prepared for the battle, and there is a " *shout in the camp.*"
Well, I hope we shall keep humble and good, as well as valiant.
Brother Alfred, the college convert, bears his trials so meekly
that it really makes his persecutors mad, and they say he
" *makes it all.*" But he puts them to silence when he speaks
for God. One of those little innocent looking sisters has gone
to East Boston. If you go there you will of course see her
and cheer her up. I learn that Brother Champlin is coming
this way soon. If you see him, stir him up to come to Yarmouth, and come yourself when you can.

We are rather beat out with care and loss of sleep, and I
have a bad cold. Pray for us.

Wife joins me in love to you and yours. Write to me if
you can spare time enough from your " fishing voyage."

Yours, in love and tribulation,

R. R. YORK.

Meeting at Biddeford. — Found a remnant
left after the devastating and withering curse
of an influence worse than Mormonism had
swept over that region. A wolf with the hy-
drophobia among sheep is to be dreaded.
Brother Boutell has been trying to nurse them,
and has done them much good of late. Next
meeting at South Berwick, on the old battle-
field of last winter. The children generally
alive; some had got wounded by the enemy,
but mean to fight their way through. A great

gathering in the evening. Some felt it duty
to be baptized. One of the selectmen led the
way. We had a good time at the water, also
in the afternoon; over one hundred were out
to meeting. This shows an interest in a thinly
settled place. In the evening over three hundred out; the house full, great interest. The
reformation of last fall has spread in various
directions. I found Elder Hall, a brother still
ready to work with all that work for the salvation of others. Our brethren need not fear
him; he will do no harm.

I must now leave for Loudon Ridge again.
On coming back to this place, a variation of
feeling and circumstances made me think of a
soldier's life. After leaving the cars I took a
wagon ride over the mountains, passing through
a chilly, snowy air; for we see here a plenty of
snowdrifts the first of May. But after riding
fifteen miles, our hearts were cheered to meet
again with Brother Batchelder's kind family,
and some ten or twelve converts in the blessed
hope, all rejoicing. Ten of them requested
baptism, four young men and six young women. This was cheering; but the devil had
suffered such a sudden loss the week before, he
commenced fortifying by circulating false reports about the work of God. Some said it was
Spiritualism, and that I had embraced it; and
every thing possible was done to head the prog-

ress of the work of God. Backsliders united
with Universalists and hypocrites in circulating
evil reports, but all this served to call the people out. Carriages from all quarters were seen
coming. It looked like a training day. Just
before meeting a brother told me the cause of
such a turnout, which put me on my guard;
but God gave me a sudden text, found in Matt.
11: 7: "What went ye out for to see?" It
took half an hour to allay the idle curiosity.
Conviction began to settle on the congregation,
when the devil saw he was losing ground,
and after such a rally. He put up a scoffing
preacher to throw in an insulting joke, which
broke the solemity of the meeting and fed the
goats. I understand he was engaged for that
purpose; at any rate he acted the part of Ba-
laam all day. God pity him! He failed at
last and left us to enjoy a blessed season in
communion with about forty that show signs
of enduring in the work of God. The season
at the baptism settled the question with every
honest Christian, that if this is a spiritual work
or brought about by Rapology, all other refor-
mations in past days were; for the power of
God settled on the congregation while Elder
Leavitt prayed for it, and did not leave it until
the ordinance was over. The first candidate I
led into the water, went in crying, and came
out shouting. This was one of the young
men alluded to above, so suddenly taken from

the devil's ranks the week before. His comrades followed him, and every one of them
gave glory to God as soon as they were resur-
rected from their watery grave. The young ladies did the same; every one came out shouting. Two lost their strength in the water.
God gave me strength to help them out, and
we had a victory in spite of the devil and his
workmen. The children feel well. I must bid
them farewell for a short time to go to my next
appointments.

I will here give extracts from three young
men who were slain by the sword of the Spirit
in Loudon Ridge. The first is from the " ringleader."

LOUDON RIDGE.

Dear Brother Munger, — Agreeable to promise I take my pen
to let you know that I mean to serve God the rest of my life.
I know that I have taken more comfort since I have tried to
serve God than when I served the devil. I am happy to-night,
for I have seen two sinners start for the kingdom. God is at
work here, and I believe that there will be more good done
yet. I will say as Brother Daniel says, that I hope God will
send the fish along so you can come and see us.

Yours, from the ringleader,

STEPHEN S. KIMBALL.

LOUDON RIDGE, May 12, 1860.

Dear Brother Munger, — God is good. He is a tender, merciful Being. I still feel to thank his holy name that he has
done that for me which man or holy angels could not do. He
has took me out of a horrible pit, and put a new song into
my mouth, even praise to the Lord. The Lord is with us.

He is to work on the minds of the people here. I feel the same determination to press my way onward to the kingdom. I want you to pray for me that I may prove faithful to the end. I hope the Lord will send the fish along so that you will come back again to Loudon Ridge.

From your brother in the Lord,

DANIEL L. MOORE.

Dear Brother Munger,—I thought I would write a few lines to let you know how I was getting along in this good way. God has been with us, and if we are faithful, I believe he will go with us to the end. We have had many blessed meetings since you left us. God has been with us by his Holy Spirit. The Lord has been very good to me, and my determination is to press forward to the kingdom.

JEREMIAH BATCHELDER.

Space will not permit an insertion of a tenth of the letters from others who have felt that the Lord is good. Here is one from a young lady, a school teacher, who has taken up the cross.

LOUDON RIDGE, May 10.

Dear Brother,—I think I have abundant reasons for believing that there is a God in Israel,—a fact I have almost doubted sometimes. Some Christians show forth such a faint copy of Christ, one is not likely to fall very much in love with it. However, I looked to religion as a last resort, when every thing else failed. Well, every thing else *did* fail, and while it left me the other alternative, it did not leave much faith to begin with. I hated to step out on so desperate a chance, and would not if I could have got rid of it. Notwithstanding I had not a hope in the world, I really hoped your meetings would not be the time after all; so much for the natural heart. I have gained a good deal of confidence in God since I started. I was so completely down it will take some time to build me up; but the Lord is doing it, and in his own time will perfect his work.

HELEN M. CHASE.

I have had other letters from Sisters Sarah Leavitt, Henrietta Batchelder, Adelaide Moore, and Sr. Batchelder, mother of some of the young converts; and also from Brother W. J. Leavitt, all of them full of thankfulness to God and resolution to press forward. God keep them.

Stopped Monday at Dover. Found a few poor sheep left alive after the wolf and his apostles had devoured all they could, as they have in every place where they have been. With the right kind of labor, there might be a reformation in Dover.

Exeter. — Found the brethren firm, but some of them in trial on account of the late destructive fire in that place, which took all the available property Brother Halcy had.

Portsmouth. — Found them well engaged. Four young men were rejoicing in God that started three weeks before, with some others, when I was there last. I was glad to hear them speak of their resolutions, and hear them pray. I learn that two of them agreed, over a bottle of rum, to take that drink, and go into meeting and ask for prayers; and they did. But instead of their drinking the rest of their rum when they left the meeting, they agreed to seal up the mouth of their bottle, with the remainder of the rum in it, as a memorial forever against drinking any more rum. This pledge holds good yet, and will as long as they serve God. I was glad to see them on my return, but did not know them until they said they started when I was there one evening, three weeks previous, on my way to Maine. This was good news, and proved true. "By the foolishness of preaching" God saves some.

Salem. — Had a very good time with Brother Berick's people. Found them very quiet. Thence to East Boston among my peculiar friends. It seemed like getting into port after five weeks' hard storm and opposition, as you see by reading this.

Truly I think Paul knew what it was to grow poor while making others rich. In the first three places I preached, there were no collections taken. My expenses had then amounted to eight dollars or more; but some places did very well, so I have received in all, for five weeks' labor and holding seventy-five meetings over my expenses, about fourteen dollars in collections. I think I have done my part at present going into out places. Am now on my way home to string my net to try fishing through the month of May. Pray that the Lord will send the fish along, so I can go out again and bear my own expenses.

NOTES BY THE WAY.

After the camp-meeting at Wilbraham, I thought it a privilege to attend meetings without so much burden on my mind. Went to the Methodist camp-meeting two days, with the intention of selecting all that was good. The two best sermons were very good, and there were some good prayer-meetings. Friday I went to the Westford meeting, and enjoyed the two days I spent there. Sunday went to South Reading. Found the church alive. Thence to South Pittsfield, to another barn meeting. Found the brethren holding on well: Some of the seed sown in the spring-time had taken root, and being watered by Brother Emerson, began to bear fruit, which roused the devil, who set cold professors to reporting all kinds of falsehoods. But I felt like bombarding the place once more in the name of God. Here I met some recruits from Portsmouth and Loudon Ridge; and although young, they helped mightily in carrying the battle forward. Some came out while the enemy growled. Others skulked when they saw persecution coming. After about a week, I left for another old battle-field of last spring. Found the company strong, with the whole armor on, not having lost a single soldier; no, not one severely wounded in six months' battle. The selectmen thought of taking care of me if I ever went back; but no officials appeared, and we had a good time serving God with the young converts from Portsmouth, who went out to see those at the Ridge. Their hearts were soon knit together like David's and Jonathan's.

Monday, by request, went back to South Pittsfield, to stop three days more and contend with Spiritualism in sheep's clothing. Then to Chichester three days. Here were a few faithful warriors who appreciated help. There was a good interest. Some received the light. Then went to Sandwich Centre. Here most of the light had been put under the bushel; but four days brought it out in sight so others saw it. God will bless them if they keep doing. This is old ground forsaken by the brethren who formerly used to preach in that region; but sectarian darkness has not killed out all the true principle. One old man said to me on my departure, "Brother M——, your visit has been worth more to me than a thousand dollars." This was the first Methodist that came into that town. He embraced the whole truth, with a good number of others, and confessed it publicly. They have established an independent free meeting every Friday evening. I hope the preaching brethren will give them a call. More good can be done in such places. There ought to be two or three good evangelists to visit such localities and feed the children.

I fear city salaries have called some from God's work. From there I went to Machiasport, Me., by especial appointment. Stopped at Portland and Yarmouth. Found the churches holding on. Took the steamer "Daniel Webster," Friday evening for Rockland. Had a hard time, sea rough. Took the boat at Rockland for Machiasport. This was still worse. The boat jumped about like a duck. Nearly all were sick. I staggered, but was not sick, except of my job. We encountered a snowstorm, and things looked dark. While I was staggering about the deck, I said to some one, I thought they had better tie the "critter" up for the night. This made me a subject for sport among the boat's crew. They all, supposing me a "greenhorn" that was frightened, had a good time, squinting and laughing at me. I felt homesick, indignant, and hungry. I found I was called the "blue surtout man." The "blue surtout" was Brother Hastings' old blue overcoat that he lent me at Portsmouth, he having a new one. I must have suffered without it in the snowstorm. Thank you, Horace, although it subjected me to notice.

It was nearly time for dinner, so I started for the cabin. Soon the bell rang, and a rush came down-stairs. I went to the further end of the table, to be as much alone as possible, and sat down at the foot of the table, as I supposed. Soon the captain and mate, and a

number of young sea captains, came down, and
seeing the old blue surtout at the head of the
table, commenced laughing, and proposed to
" tie the critter up," etc. Soon one said, " Put
on steam and run away from danger, for this
man is scared," referring to me. I stopped
eating and said, " Gentlemen, you had better
keep your gas for some one younger than I am.
In fifty-four years I have seen a great many people and some fools." This stopped their fun.
I then told them that I had seen the salt water
before, for I had been the length of Long Island
Sound and back three times, and wasn't sick
nor scared. I then left for the deck. It appeared that after I left, one of the oldest seamen said, " Boys, that old surtout man knows
more about the world than all the rest of us.
He has doubled the ' Horn ' three times. He
has come the game on us." Soon I had company enough inquiring about my voyages. I
kept in the dark about it, only saying I had been
the length of Long Island Sound three times.
This made it certain that I had doubled the
" Horn," and I was soon honored unexpectedly,
treated with respect, and got to my appointment Sunday morning in good time. Some of
the crew looked strange when they saw that
same old blue coat go into the desk; but God
worked; sinners were converted; the whole place
stirred. The Baptists opened their doors, and
I preached three times. The work was started

there. Some were converted and others convicted. God moved the whole population. I
consented to stay the second sabbath. The
work increased all the week. Sunday, six requested baptism. This was new and unexpected to the people in that backslidden place.
Sunday evening there was the greatest interest
I have seen for years. I presume there were
fifty under conviction the second Sunday evening. But I had to leave it where it was; to
stay another week I could not, and the boat left
Mondays only.

These brethren have held on without any
preaching but once for over two years, and then
Brother Lenfest called on them to see how the
seed looked that he sowed five years before. I
felt that my visit was greatly appreciated, by
them, and blessed to the conversion of a good
many sinners. It got among the seamen. One
mate of a vessel and his brother were among
the converts that were baptized. I left them,
probably never to meet again on earth. I hope
the preaching brethren will call on them.

This ended a tour of eight weeks. I had a
rough time coming home on the boats; was
hindered two days for the storm to abate. I
took my line and caught fish enough for the
whole boat's crew one meal. So I became
noted again, and got two meals free. I had to
stay at Rockland over night. At six Wednesday morning I was awakened by the earth-

quake, which said the whole earth groans for deliverance, which will come soon.

I did not think of noticing this trip till some suggested it after hearing some of these incidents. There was a theft of thirty-eight dollars on board, but the energetic efforts of the officers detected the thief. Three men were on board in irons, going to state prison, one for five years. So we had a variety, all showing that wickedness is not at an end. Let us keep doing as long as God is willing to show mercy to sinners. I think it safe to say, I have seen fifty start to serve God this time out. Thank the Lord, children.

The following extracts from letters from three sisters and their brother in Machiasport show that the Lord has been at work there also: —

MACHIAS, Oct. 23, 1860.

Dear Brother in Christ, — It is with pleasure that I address you. I am enjoying myself quite well at the present. Oh, had I known the love of Jesus I would not have lived in sin and rebellion as long as I have. But I ought to thank him, for he has opened my eyes, and brought me into his glorious light. Pray for me that my faith fail not.

MARGARET C. WESCOTT.

Dear Brother in Christ, — Agreeable to your request I now write to you. I am still trying to serve my Lord and Saviour. Oh, if I had tried to serve him before, I should have taken so much pleasure; but I ought to thank him for his goodness to me, in showing me my sins.

SARAH E. WESCOTT.

Dear Brother Munger, — I love my Lord as well as ever,

and I mean to praise him while I live. Pray for me that I may ever be found watching.

LOWESER G. WESCOTT.

Dear Brother, — We have many battles to fight, but our enemies hang themselves as soon as they get rope enough. I had a combat with one of the old Cain family. He said he believed in Christ's literal coming ; but before he got through he said it was to be a spiritual kingdom. We should be pleased to have some one come and stop with us a while.

STEPHEN O. WESCOTT.

From Bro. J. F. Cotton.

I was present when the invitation to visit Machiasport was pressingly extended to Brother Munger by Captain Abraham Johnson of that place. Since Brother Munger returned, Brother Johnson, in my presence, congratulated the author of this book on the success of his mission, and bore testimony to the goodness of God in reviving his work in that portion of his vineyard.

JNO. F. COTTON.

I have now brought the narrative of my labors to an end for the present. I thank God for his mercies to myself as well as others among whom I have labored and sojourned. I would admonish all who are in the good way to stand fast, and those who are without Christ in their hearts, the hope of glory, to lose no time in accepting the call of grace. Time is short, the kingdom is at hand! Let us be prepared with lamps trimmed and lights burning in hopeful watching for the bridegroom.

USEFUL RECIPES.

The following recipes may be relied on.

EXTRACT OF LOBELIA.

Taken as an Emetic for Cramp, Fever, Fits, Asthma, or as an Antidote.

The best thing, I think, that has ever been discovered for an emetic, is the new way of preparing Lobelia in the form of Extract. It is perfectly safe and thorough; and the best nervine I know of is a small dose on going to bed; also, for cramp, fevers, and fits. No family would be without it if they knew its value. It is the best remedy for asthma I ever saw tried, and also for poison of any kind.

HOT DROPS.

Hot Drops are excellent to break up a cold; also for cramp, dysentery, and cholera, sores, sprains, and rheumatism. To one gallon of new rum (high wines) add one-half a pound of gum of myrrh (pulverized), two ounces of golden seal, two ounces of bayberry bark, two ounces powdered rhubarb, two ounces cayenne pepper, put into a jug and set it into a kettle of boiling water until the liquor boils, always leaving the cork out. When it has boiled fifteen minutes, pour it out into a vessel, and when cool strain it. Add half a pint of good molasses, and bottle it. One table-spoonful of the hot drops is a dose for an adult. Those who make it should be careful and not carry a light near the steam while boiling.

TREATMENT OF FELON.

There are three kinds of felon, the *Whitlow, Frog,* and *Bone-felon.*

RECEIPT FOR MY MOTHER'S POULTICE. — A gill of the inner bark of basswood, scraped fine, half a pint of hot water, steep half an hour, add the yolk of one egg, and a piece of white pine pitch about the size of a walnut. Stir until well mixed, then add wheat flour enough to make it of proper thickness. The egg and flour must not be added till nearly cold. Put it on while warm, and change as often as it becomes dry. Use while fresh. Before applying the poultice soak the felon in hot soap suds. This poultice is as good for any other sore as for the felon. If basswood cannot be got, pulverized slippery elm will do.

BOILS, CARBUNCLES, ANT-HILLS, ETC.

Whole mustard or burdock seed, taken, a teaspoonful at a time, is good to purge the impurities of the blood, which is the cause of those troublesome neighbors. The best external application for a boil, that I ever tried, is a thin slice of salt pork laid on the sore. It will ease the pain and allay the inflammation.

FOR PUTRID SORES.

Take two drachms of saltpetre, dissolve in half a pint of water, and wash the sore two or three times a day, at the same time using gentle purgatives.

BURNS.

Make an ointment from the green of elder. Dress the sores with it, changing often. Yet I believe there is nothing as good for a burn as cold water. Always keep the wound covered with a cloth, wet with water, until the fire is out, which will take some time if the burn is bad. Water will put out fire, if applied upon us, as truly as on a building. The same remedy is good for frozen limbs.

FOR CRAMP FITS.

Bathe freely with warm water, at the same time giving warming medicines. If people are forewarned, a dose of strong catnip tea will generally prevent fits.

FOR FEVER AND AGUE.

From J. F. Cotton.

Two table-spoonfuls of coffee, boiled in a pint of water, down to half a pint. Into this liquor squeeze a lemon, and take on the morning of the day usual for the chills to come on, until vomiting ensues.

FOR GRAVEL OR DISORDERS OF THE KIDNEYS.

From J. F. Cotton.

Take equal parts of pine-pitch, saltpetre, sulphur, and charcoal ; make into pills half the size of buck shot, and take two before each meal.

AN EXCELLENT FAMILY MEDICINE.

THE *Remedy* for Fevers, Dyspepsia, Headache, Bowel Complaints, Jaundice, Costiveness, Liver Complaint, and all Bilious Difficulties, is

DO NOT BE WITHOUT IT!

DR. PIERCE'S
INDIAN RESTORATIVE BITTERS.

THOUSANDS of persons have been prostrated by *Fevers,
Dysentery, Cholera Morbus, Diarrhœa,* and bilious difficulties,
the result of which has often proved fatal for the want of some
seasonable, reliable, effective medicine, one which, while it
cleanses the stomach, bowels, and blood, removing unhealthy
matter, expelling the cause of disease, *restores* the vital ener-
gies, imparting health and strength to the whole system.
Such a medicine is Dr. Pierce's Indian Restorative Bitters.

We have letters from a large number of well-known persons who have
used this medicine, from which we give a few extracts:—

The best family medicine I know of is Doctor Geo. Pierce's
Indian Restorative Bitters. It is safe in all cases, effectual
and easy in its operation. I can honestly recommend it to
my friends to be the best and safest article to keep on hand.
I know it after twelve years' acquaintance. I do consider it a
duty and privilege to speak in its favor. It seems almost in-
dispensable to families that have used it. Probably more
recommendations could be got for the utility of this medicine
than any other in the world. I know what it is and what it
has done, and what it *will* do if used according to the directions.   HIRAM MUNGER.

From Rev. E. T. TAYLOR, Pastor of Seamen's Bethel, well-known
as "Father Taylor."

We have used it in our family for a number of years, and
have always found it to answer your recommendations. We
should be very unwilling to be without it. It has relieved me
from severe attacks of Bowel Complaints, Dyspepsia, and
Costiveness. I would take it with me were I going to sea,
and also were I to travel. It might save me from detention,
and in my opinion it would be well for others to do the same.

Elder Daniel P. Pike, Newburyport, Mass, Oct. 31, 1856, says:—

"Dr. PIERCE,—In my family, for the last twelve years,
your Indian Restorative Bitters has taken the place of purga-
tive pills, and other nostrums destructive to the human system.
It should be in the medicine chest of every family."

I have used Dr. Pierce's Bitters, and consider it unequalled
as a family medicine. And also, from my knowledge of what
seamen require, I hold it the best remedy for those maladies
peculiar to the Tropics and the Southern States.
                          JNO. F. COTTON, Boston, Mass.

Elder F. H. Derick says: —

DR. PIERCE, — Of all the medical preparations in the shape of Bitters, Pills, etc., I pronounce yours unqualifiedly the best of any with which I have ever been acquainted. Having thoroughly tested the medicine myself, I do the more confidently recommend it to any and all who may be affected with Jaundice, Loss of Appetite, Constipation, Bilious Colic, Dyspepsia, etc. In all Bilious difficulties I believe this medicine is unsurpassed.

Elder A. Hale, formerly editor of the *Advent Herald*, says: —

For Fever, Dysentery, Colic, Dyspepsia, or any of the numerous intestinal derangements, I consider your Bitters so far superior to any thing else to which I have any knowledge, and so necessary to the health of my family, that I should consider myself inexcusable to be without it.

Elder M. Grant, editor of *The World's Crisis*, says: —

We do not believe much in drugs and medicines, but those who have used Dr. Geo. Pierce's Indian Restorative Bitters, do say, that for Dyspepsia, Fevers, Dysentery, Bilious Complaints, Costiveness, and the various intestinal derangements, it is the best medicine that they have ever used — effecting *cures* when various other medicines have failed. And from our knowledge of the proprietors of this valuable medicine, we are sure that they would not present to the public any other than an article worthy of its full confidence; and that they rely upon *facts only*, which they have in abundance, to demonstrate the *truth* of the superiority of their medicine.

Dr. Geo. Pierce's Indian Restorative Bitters.

We would call particular attention to this truly most valuable medicine. From our own knowledge, and from the testimony of many who have experienced its beneficial effects, we most fully recommend it to the community as a remedy worthy their confidence—a most effectual one to cleanse the Stomach, Bowels, and Blood, and to breaking up fevers, thus preventing serious illness, as well as curing it in more advanced stages. We regard it as a medicine sure to save much sickness and expense wherever used. —*Herald of Gospel Liberty.*

PREPARED BY

GEO. PIERCE & CO., LOWELL, MASS.

For sale by Geo. T. Adams, at his Hat, Cap, and Clothing House, 167 Hanover Street, Boston, Mass., and by leading Medicine Dealers in New England.

WHITTEN'S GOLDEN SALVE.

THIS is a very choice healing remedy, for the cure of Sores and Humors of all kinds, and also for Piles, Spinal disease, Rheumatism, Swellings, Boils, Chilblains, and all grievous accidents.

The Golden Salve has become a popular curative throughout the country. Standing upon its own merits, and the cures it has performed, it has attained a reputation as a healing agent, hitherto unattained by any remedy known.

I feel great pleasure in offering my testimony to the great healing properties of this invaluable salve. I am prone to look with distrust upon all " puffed " medicines, and until I have tested them *myself*, or received favorable testimony from persons of unquestionable honesty, I have little confidence in them. For a considerable time before I tried it, I read innumerable paragraphs in the daily papers lauding it to the skies. But I paid little attention to it till the dreadful catastrophe of the Pemberton Mills brought its soothing and healing powers before the community. When scores of bruised, mangled, and scorched victims were dragged out of the burning ruins, Mr. Whitten came to the rescue with his money, and yet more precious ointment; and many from that day bore testimony to its qualities, who perhaps never would have known of it, save in name. I was among the last named. I read a few of the many vouchers of its efficacy, and resolved to try it. My wife was suffering with broken breast; and the salve brought her relief. I was troubled with piles, and the salve at once assuaged the irritation. I let a neighbor, whose child was suffering from a bad chafe, have some, and the infant was shortly cured. Space will not allow me to say all that I might upon this subject; but I would recommend it to the notice of every housekeeper in the country; and more particularly to those who, by their position, cannot at all times command the services of a doctor. To *sailors* it would be of incalculable benefit, and not one of them should go to sea without a supply in his chest, if it can be found.

JNO. F. COTTON.

From Elder Hiram Munger.

The Salve that is here introduced I have tried myself, and seen its effects on others, until I am satisfied it is the best Family Salve in use. Try it and you will know what I say is true. I would not insert a thing in this work, that was not thoroughly tested, for love or money. The Salve is the best I ever used. I have been engaged in the healing art for twenty-four years, and have found nothing so good.

H. MUNGER.

In Boston it can be found at the establishments of M. S. BURR & Co., 36 Tremont St., GEO. C. GOODWIN & Co., 11 Marshall St., WEEKS & POTTER, 154 Washington St., J. F. COTTON, 167 Hanover St., and at nearly all Druggists and Stores in the city or country. Made only by

C. P. WHITTEN, Lowell, Mass.

WHITE'S
SPECIFIC REMEDY FOR DYSPEPSIA.

DYSPEPSIA shows itself not only in a painful pressure in the pit of the stomach, where the seat of disease is, but in all the varied forms of bodily derangement, such as headache, in its different forms, neuralgia, loss of appetite, sometimes too great an appetite, wanting to eat often, or all the time, vomiting the food, sour stomach, flatulence, constipation of the bowels, diarrhœa, piles, weakness of the limbs, rheumatism, general debility, kidney complaints, unpleasant feeling about the region of the heart, palpitation of the heart (often mistaken for disease of the heart), cold feet, restless sleep, nightmare, more tired in the morning on rising than on going to bed, sometimes unable to sleep at all, and at other times wanting to sleep too much, frightful dreams, faintness, wanting to be eating something, though the stomach be full, nervous diseases (in all their distressing features) of body and mind.

This remedy for dyspepsia is composed of articles known to be directly adapted to meet the case of every one who may be afflicted by this malady. It is perfectly safe in all cases. Knowing the nature of the composition, and preparing the remedy ourselves, we are confident that, with proper regard for the directions, it will effect a cure of this dreadful disease. It will remove all Humors from the system, and so assist nature to throw off the morbid secretions, as that health shall be the result.

☞ Put up in 25 cents to $1.00 packages, and sent by mail to any part of the United States free of extra expense.

To be had by addressing J. F. COTTON, *Crisis Office*, 167 Hanover Street, Boston, Mass., or the manufacturer and proprietor,

J. S. WHITE, East Boston, Mass.

www.ingramcontent.com/pod-product-compliance
Lightning Source LLC
Chambersburg PA
CBHW030134030726
47498CB00007B/2703